STATIONS

ALSO *by* NICK MULGREW

the myth of this is that we're all in this together
(poems, uHlanga, 2015)

NICK MULGREW

STATIONS

STORIES

DAVID PHILIP PUBLISHERS
CAPE TOWN
2016

Stations

First published in South Africa by David Philip Publishers
6 Spin Street, Cape Town, 8001

ISBNs

978-1-4856-2484-4 (PRINT)
978-1-4856-2485-1 (EPUB)
978-1-4856-2486-8 (MOBI)

Edited by Helen Moffett
Cover illustration by skullboy | Cover design by Louis de Villiers
Typeset by Nick Mulgrew

Versions of some stories in this collection were first published in the following: "Ponta do Ouro" in *Feast, Famine & Potluck* (Short Story Day Africa, S.A., 2013); "Gala Day" in *Prufrock* 5 (S.A., 2014); "Turning" in *Adults Only* (Burnet Media/ National Arts Festival, S.A., 2014); "Stations" in *Terra Incognita* (Short Story Day Africa, S.A., 2014); "Posman" in the *White Review* (U.K., 2015); "Restaurant" in *New Contrast* 170 (S.A., 2015); "Mariannhill, in the Garden" in the *Stockholm Review* (Sweden, 2015); "1-HR FOTO" in *Ons Klyntji* 21 (S.A., 2015). A version of "Daughter" appeared on *Visual Verse* in 2013.

The author would like to thank Jennifer Jacobs, Efemia Chela, Amy Uzzell, Adbul-Malik Sibabalwe Oscar Masinyana, and Sindiwe Magona for their input to these stories, and to Dušanka Stojaković for her support of this book in general.

For Eileen
For Jimmy
For Josephine
For Mhoira
For Les
For Ronald
For Ernest

CONTENTS

ATHLONE TOWERS

I don't know why I ever let you in. You were on borrowed time from the first, and I was going to let you down. I knew it. You didn't. You still believed in this thing we might have had. Perhaps I should have spared you the pain, or at least the bother. But somehow I hoped. I had this image in my mind, of a tree that had managed to grow its roots through tarmac. That's how I hoped this would end up. In something that would grow. In something that would not die.

I remember coming back home after making the trip to see you the last time. I was listening to *Hatful of Hollow* and lying on the floor on my fake Persian carpet with the lights off, in a way I thought would be fitting for this kind of moment, like a scene in a coming-of-age film, or the part of a novel in which a big realisation is made. And I remember saying to myself, convincing myself to love you again, to make the effort again, thinking: don't let go of this feeling, don't let go of this feeling, don't let go of this feeling. I thought I could, I don't know, force myself to change. That I could write my own myths. You'd accused me of being a flip-flopper. Of being inexact. And I wanted to prove that you wrong about that.

Now I regret not discarding that feeling as soon as I felt it. And really that's the only regret I have. It could have saved you a lot of grief.

I remember how you dropped me off at the airport on my way back to East London, and how on the way you told me that the cooling towers in Athlone were to be demolished that afternoon. And as we passed them on the highway, all slick with rain, I remarked on how tall they were. It was an obvious thing to say. I was full of obvious things to say that day: "I'll miss you"; "Maybe it'll work out"; "This hurts".

I still remember what the towers looked like, especially that day: these huge funnels of concrete ringed with bands, flanked by a thin rainbow from a now-distant storm, a disturbance of tracksuited men like ants at their foundations. You were telling me how they were going to bring the towers down. You described it like a news report. Seven thousand tiny charges, set off in a fraction of a second.

And I thought, Jesus, how easy a metaphor this would be for this moment, for you and me. A metaphor about, I don't know, how there were these things – these looming, imposing things that had been built on the landscape on our hearts, or something asinine like that, and that now they were going to be demolished.

Jesus, it writes itself. People were coming from all over town – from Paarl and Worcester and all the fraying edges of the Cape – to watch. And I was leaving right as it was happening. You were hoping to rush up to Rhodes Mem after dropping me off at the airport. I don't remember our goodbye, but I remember hearing afterwards how you missed seeing the towers come down. It was only a matter of minutes: the demolition team set off the charges too early. Articles were written about it, about people still setting up their cameras, or talking to friends, filling that unbearable gap in time before something big and meaningful is scheduled to happen.

I can't help thinking that seeing it happen might have brought you closure. That it might have been some indication that life has its resonances and its syncronisations, that sometimes things still happen plainly just for you, in a world of unfurled images, of unmatched imaginings, of things scribbled in your tiny knot-writing in your bed in the early morning. Of wishes given over in silence, under a moon still risen over whichever place, whichever hemisphere you find yourself in, yearning for something you could put into words.

But as it happened, you were still in your Suzuki, racing past the university, and when you got through the forests of oak and pine to the top of the hill, all you saw was this cloud of dust, these giant things already deflated and flopped in on each other.

A landscape had changed forever, and you hadn't seen it happen.

TURNING

I

I used to live in this little yellow apartment in a little yellow apartment block just off Cross Street. The wooden floors creaked, the way wooden floors do.

I didn't have a car. This was a source of great anxiety. Grahamstown is not a walker's town, after all. The distances between places are short, sure, but the drivers are erratic and the sidewalks uneven. Few things in life are worse than being five draughts down at the Rat and Parrot and remembering you have to walk home. You visualise the walk, work out the shortest route – down back New Street, left up Somerset, past High, left down Beaufort (three blocks), up the hill on Glanville and over to Cross – and hope the weather won't change. Most nights it didn't.

When it rained, I jogged home. Just about the only exercise I got in three years in Grahamstown was from running home at 4 a.m., down the middle of Beaufort Street, with my house keys clasped like claws between my knuckles. One night I sprinted the entire way home, light-headed from spirits and wary of muggers, only to collapse on the grass outside my block. I was woken up just after sunrise by a neighbour. My face was wet with dew.

You knew nothing of the dangers of running home. You had an old white Ford – an Escort with no hubcaps – that you drove home no matter how much you drank. You failed a breathalyser once and paid the cop to let you off. Of course it worked.

You kept a bra in the cubbyhole and your hockey boots on the back seat. We never kissed on the back seat. We kissed sitting in the front seats once, after we'd eaten KFC and were looking over town from the Monument. It was sometime in May, late at night. I remember the dull yellow glow, the strings of streetlights pulsing through the fog. There was the cathedral, towering through, disrupting the flatness of the tin-roofed houses lining the valley below, its spire the only indication that this might be a city and not a backwater town before us. I remember you saying this place could be beautiful. Could. We twisted over the gearstick in the half-light, your tongue in my mouth, my hand up your shirt.

And at that moment, for some reason I still can't place, I wanted to reach between us and release the handbrake, just to see what would happen.

I still think I should have found out.

II

You know I never loved you.

III

I grew up in this tiny suburb in PE called Brooke's Hill. Nobody's ever heard of it, but everyone's gone past it.

We lived up on a road called Kings Close. Taxi drivers never knew where it was, so we had to explain on the phone: "up La Roche, turn at the Catholic church on Happy Valley, then up the hill behind the Kelway. Yes, *behind* it." It wouldn't have been a problem if we didn't have to call a taxi whenever we wanted to go anywhere – my mom refused to learn to drive until she was forty.

My mom's Indian. Or of Indian descent. She's Pietermaritzburgian, I suppose, or whatever the adjective is for someone from Pietermaritzburg. She loves silver jewellery and doesn't wear makeup. My dad's white; grew up in Walmer and went to Grey, third-team rugby, the whole package. They met at Rhodes, married young and had me not very long after. My dad is lumberjack handsome. And me: well, I look strange.

But I was good enough for you. You liked my uneasy tone, my origami construction.

We also met at Rhodes. I saw you one night at the Rat during my second year. You'd just moved in with Jules, an old school friend of mine. He thought you were pretty. I'd never seen anything like you – auburn, slinky, gap-toothed. You said you were from Mafikeng. I pretended I knew where that was.

I bought you two Heinekens. Afterwards you let me walk you down New Street to a club with a gaggle of your friends. The air inside was damp, the floor sticky from spilled drinks: Black Labels, cane and cream sodas, ten-rand brandy and Coke. All the specials. I tried to flirt with you. I banged the bottom of my third or fourth bottle of Label on the top of yours to try and make the beer spray out onto you. Instead,

I shattered your bottle. Beer soaked your shoes. Glass stuck out your thumb. You bled into the sleeve of your jersey.

I stormed into the men's bathroom, clambered over someone vomiting in the cubicle – it might have been a woman – and grabbed a roll of toilet paper.

"I'm really, really sorry," I said once I'd fought back through the crowd. I wrapped your thumb. "I know what I'm doing," I assured you. "My mom's a nurse." I expected you to pull away from me.

You did the opposite.

IV

We had this old professor in the history department who was convinced the world was about to end. He gave fire-and-brimstone lectures on American imperialism, Monsanto, the death of Gaia – that sort of thing. He was somewhat famous back in the day, his reputation cemented by an argument he'd sparked with a couple of British historians, who argued that Shaka Zulu was a warlord. The old professor said Shaka wasn't. He said the way Shaka was usually portrayed – as a fearmonger, an object of terror – was a colonialist construct. The British said he was revisionist. I never picked a side, but the whole thing ended up having its own page on Wikipedia, so I guess it was pretty serious.

Anyway, while I only took history for a few months, I'd always see this professor at Pick n Pay on Saturday mornings. A sad-looking man, a bit clown-like too. He wore these bright lacy waistcoats smothered in kitsch African motifs. His face was a permanent frown. He usually carried a one-kilo tin of Milo under his arm.

A res-mate from first year told me a rumour that the professor's partner had had an affair with someone else in the history department. It made sense, but I still couldn't understand how he could go through that much Milo.

I used to run into you at Pick n Pay, too. You liked chutney Nik-Naks. Your basket was usually full of them. Nik-Naks and tinned tomatoes. You ate penne and tomatoes every night for dinner. You said you liked it. It kept you sort of skinny. I was OK with that.

One Saturday, I pointed out the old professor to you. You said that you thought it was beautiful that he could feel that sort of pain about love at his age.

"But he's been married to that woman for decades," I said.

"Most people don't get to love someone for decades," you said.

"Fair enough," I said.

ᔕ

We had sex for the first time that night.

I had offered to help you with a linguistics assignment, a simple phonetics tutorial, at your res room. I remember you said you had trouble with vowels, a problem only a language student could have.

You struggled with phonetic charts; how the phonetic notation of vowels corresponds to where in our mouth we give voice to them. We distinguished between diphthongs and monophthongs; the ways in which we sustain and change the sounds in our mouths with a flick of our tongues or the slight undulation of our throats and palates. I told you how South Africans had, over the years, managed to elide all of our approximant "r" sounds – how we turned 'car' into 'kah', and 'barrier' into 'barriya'. I told you how we reduced all the subtleness of vowels to this simple schwa, this "uh" sound, this [ə].

It felt like I had talked for hours. I thought I had covered everything. Then you asked me how rounded and unrounded vowels worked.

"It's easy," I said, shifting the notes around on your bed. "It has to do with labialisation. You just have to round your lips a bit."

"Oh *really*." You drawled, uncrossing your legs. "Like how, exactly?"

I sighed. We'd already gone through this. I puckered and pointed to my lips, about to perfectly demonstrate to you the difference between an unrounded front close-mid [e] and a rounded front close-mid [ø], when you kissed me.

I put my hand on your hip as you curled over me. I slid my hand upwards, under the inner fleece of your hoodie. You weren't wearing a bra. Your nipples grew taut under my fumbling touch. The papers crumpled beneath us. You ran your fingers through my terrier hair, kissed soft fricatives on my ears, drew circles on my scalp. You tasted of rooibos and mint.

I slipped a finger under the elastic of your shorts, feeling for the soft brush of your hair, that warm split between your legs. You gasped [ɑ]. You pulled off my jeans and took me into your mouth.

It all happened so fast. I fished in my wallet for the condom I had until now kept as a joke, while you knelt and held onto the metal frame of your single bed, your hair running in curls down the nape of your neck. You turned your head sideways, towards me. I could have counted the dimples in your spine.

I wasn't sure what I could do with you, so I asked you to go on top. You obliged, curving over me, and pressed on me deep and slow. Even then I knew I wouldn't last long, so I tried to distract myself. In my head I tried to place the shape of your moans on the IPA vowel chart. You started at unrounded back close-mid [o], then shifted to rounded back close-mid [ɤ] when you picked up the pace. Open central [ä] – ah, ah, ah. A vocal rhythm to the soft slap of bodies. You whimpered, engraved grids into my chest, charting our movement across them with your nails.

You pulled on the back of my head, bringing my face up toward yours. Bilabial nasal [m] as we kissed again. You were metallic, molten, mineral – something new and warm. I was short of breath, gripping the soft skin of your hips, feeling the chafe of your res-standard sheets on my heels. I groaned and bucked, as I felt I was supposed to.

"Shh," you said. Voiceless post-alveolar fricative, [ʃ]. "Relax. Let me do the work."

You straightened your back. Now I could see you. Now I could see your breasts, their knocking, their rose gilding. Now I could see your soft collar of freckles, fading into your shoulders. Now I could see the belly ring I had not expected to see.

Your bed scraped on the linoleum as you jackhammered me into submission. I thanked God we were on the ground floor. You let off soft sounds, [ɞ, ɞ, ɞ]. Rounded central open-mid – oh, oh, oh. Again I started to buck. This time you let off an ooh. Rounded back close, [u].

After a couple of moments, you began to touch yourself. You rolled on me, oceanic and plump.

"It's the only way I can come," you said.

"Fair enough," I gasped between strokes.

You flung your head back and bared your teeth.

[ə], [ə], [ə].

My heart raced anapestic.

Schwa, schwa, schwa.

V

I was ten when I was almost abducted at the Boardwalk. Long story short: a man tried to pull me away from the games arcade while my parents were finishing dinner. He was fifty-ish and wore an anorak and corduroy pants. He stank of something I didn't know. He squatted down next to me and kissed my hand by way of greeting, scraping his moustache against my fingers. It took me a moment to find the air in my lungs to scream, and a moment more for the security guard to find where my screams were coming from. When the man let go of my hand, I ran.

I tripped over my slops on the way out of the arcade and fell on the tarmac. It was at that point I started to cry. By the time I got back to the restaurant, my parents were settling the bill. I tried to spit out what had happened, but all they saw were my bloodied knees.

"Oh dear," my mom said, squatting down next to me. "I'm sorry." She kissed my hand.

My dad picked me up and ran his fingers through my hair. "Come on," he said. "You're big now, son. You don't have to cry."

I looked over my dad's shoulders, over the artificial lake, where the lights of the casino played among the lily pads and the reeds, and thought I saw the corduroyed man being taken away by the guard into a car park.

I was going to tell my parents what happened when we got home, after my mom had finished slathering Mercurochrome on my knees like it was sunscreen, but I never got round to it.

VI

There are twenty-something spires in Grahamstown. Each is connected to a church. Some are connected to a school connected to a church, but connected to a church all the same.

The Cathedral of St Michael and St George has the tallest spire in the country, and a host of bells that shatter the Sunday air. St Patrick's is red-bricked and stout, sunken into the dip of Hill Street. Commemoration Methodist rises gnarled over the war memorial, stain-glassed and gothic, stuck between Birch's department store and the Dunlop tyre shop.

These are the churches that dominate the sky. But there are more churches – churches without spires – that hold dominion over the earth. The charismatics, those whose memberships congregate in vacant school halls; those who hand out flyers on street corners in Joza and Fingo; those churches filled with voices polychromatic.

But more holy is the room that holds our bed, the posts between which our most fervent praise of God comes, thick from our lips.

How does one deserve this? How can one deserve the way everything was constructed, from dirt and ash and rock, all to place this person here with me? How worlds and universes and stardust were broken up and subsided here, in the midst of brick and sheet-roofing and oak; how two bodies of water and carbon and phosphorous and bone fight here with all their will to inhabit the same points of space and time as the other.

I hadn't prayed in all my life until the night you fell asleep, afterwards, next to me.

VII

Let me tell you about this dream I had about you and this girl.

You kissed each other on a mattress in the middle of this huge, dark room. She was on top of you, under a thin fleece blanket. Your legs knotted together, your hands exploring each other. Her skin began to melt into yours. It dripped like unction onto the span of your breasts.

I floated somewhere in a corner, detached, naked for some reason. I couldn't hear either. Instead, the entire world was rendered as you and her. When you gasped, great clouds of colour rushed from beneath the blanket. Moans slithered kaleidoscopic from your mouths. Tendrils of warmth bound you to the bed, trellising up the walls, cross-hatching the ceiling. The room pulsed with light as she kissed you.

I tried to call out to you, but I could not speak. I reached into my mouth and pulled out innumerable strings of thread. I kept reaching and pulling, reaching and pulling as I saw your lips fuse together. I beat my chest and felt my ribs cave in: I was stuffed with cotton. I stuck my fingers down my throat, yanking out my insides, aching to say something, anything. At last I rid myself of my innards. I let out a shout. Your communion cracked electric.

I woke on the floor with my fingers in my mouth.

∽

You never actually told me outright. I just sort of worked it out. One week in October, we were sleeping together. The next, you were spending your nights with her. The next you told me you'd kissed her as a joke. You said she liked you. She studied botany, I think, so I didn't know much about her. Departmental divisions. She wore this army jacket and hung around at the sports bar on Scott Street. She bought my friends drinks once.

"You read about bullshit like this in *FHM*," Jules said down at the Rat, "how it's like a guy's worst nightmare. It's because of you, obviously" – he chuckled over his beer – "you didn't know how to please her. It's because you were a virgin before you met her."

I gulped down the rest of my draught. It had gone warm. "Thanks," I said. "*Real* comforting. Wasn't as if you had a chance with her in the first place."

"You know what I mean, though." He spun his coaster between his fingertips. "Sorry. It's just weird."

"That's the thing," I said. "I tried to look it up on the Internet, but nobody really tells you what it's like – or, like, what to *do* – when someone you're with figures out they're gay."

"You'd think there'd be *some*thing," Jules said. He looked over my shoulder to catch the score. Goalless. "You know, you'd think there'd at least be some chick whining on her blog or some shitty thinkpiece in the *Atlantic* or something."

"Yeah. But it looks like it never happens to anyone."

"Except that it happened to you," Jules said.

"Except that it happened to me."

VIII

"That never happened," you said, running your fingers through my hair. "There's no games arcade at the Boardwalk."

IX

Here, autumn turns to winter with little ceremony. One day you're wearing a T-shirt and shorts, and the next you put on a K-Way zip-up and commit to holing yourself up in your bedroom for two months. You call your friends with access to the uni's file-sharing network. You beg them to come over and drop off episodes of *Skins* on a flash drive. They oblige.

Warmth is a commodity. You buy a shitty space heater from Checkers and it breaks as soon as the guarantee runs out. So you infest the bars, drink red wine and let it heat your blood. Then you move onto quarts of Label. Clearance sale at the student union. Fifty-cent vodka shots. Pay to watch shitty metal bands just so you can get the specials – it works out. One night you give your gloves to a street kid prowling New Street. He'll probably have them stolen by another kid later that night. One night you punch a white first-year in the face when he calls you a coolie. One night you end up in your girlfriend's bed with a bust lip and a cold, trying to decipher her tattoos while she sleeps.

"So what does that even mean?" you ask her in the morning.

She rubs sleep from her eyes. "Hm?"

"*Ne estas kialo*. What does it mean?"

"'There is no why.' It's Esperanto. I got it during matric rage."

You shift on your side. "What on earth is Esperanto? Some weird Limpopo thing? Thought they spoke Tswana or something up there."

"North West. Not Limpopo."

"Regardless."

She sighs. "It's a language some Polish guy came up with in the nineteenth century. Someone who dreamed of a language that would transcend all the rest."

"Ever the linguist," you say, circling the words on the topography of her ribs. "So, like a language for the world? Like Babel or some shit?"

"Sure, you could call it that."

"Never heard of it."

She touches your lip, asks if it's still sore.

You'll ignore her and persist: "So why'd you get the tat?"

"Ne estas kialo."

"Cute. Real cute."

"Sorry," she pushes you onto your back and shifts her body onto yours. You feel her warmth, her heartbeat through her chest. "Tell you the truth, I saw it on someone's MySpace page during matric. I found the whole thing romantic back then, I guess. A world in which we could all understand each other."

"That would be nice. But I think it'd boring too, wouldn't it?"

"I guess." She scrunches up her face. "It'd just get rid of a lot of problems."

She tries to kiss you, but it's too sore to bear.

x

You broke up with me while we sat in the front seats of your Ford. It was 1am on a Tuesday. We sat under a flickering streetlight on Cross. We'd been drinking at the Rat, sitting at an indoor picnic table with your friends, who all insisted on smoking. Of course you drove me home.

I asked you if you wanted to come inside. You said this – *we* – had to end. I asked when, and you said now, and I asked if you were sure, and you said yes. And so I tried to kiss you with my stitched lip and you turned your cheek and I was in my bed within the minute, masturbating so I could fall asleep. That didn't work, so I tried again when I could conjure enough snapshots of you naked to get myself up again. But that didn't work either.

It's hard to say what I felt. There was a storm outside like a storm in heaven, and the wind blew in Grahamstown like the wind in Grahamstown blows, and my building shook in the wind the way old buildings shake. It's hard to say what I felt, but it felt like it would have been better if you were in my bed to share that storm with me.

I took a bus to P.E. later in the morning, a Greyhound caught at the Frontier Hotel an hour after booking a ticket at the High Street Checkers. I sat next to a woman eating half a rotisserie chicken with her fingers for brunch.

I stayed with my parents until Friday. On the return trip, the bus hit a goat. When we stopped to inspect the damage, a man near the front stood up and asked the attendant if he could put the animal in the luggage store so he could cook it later for his family. I didn't hear the rest of the conversation, but I don't think he got his wish.

Back in Grahamstown, Jules told me you'd been staying over at the other girl's house. She'd even taken you to a digs formal. Jules tried to convince me you hadn't hooked up. I didn't believe him: "Every couple fucks after a digs formal," I said. "That's the whole point." I phoned you and called you a dyke. Jules thought that you were a LUG: a Lesbian Until Graduation. Eventually I managed to laugh about it, and as winter turned to spring I spent all my time rewriting essays and pretending not to care about your latest bout of self-discovery.

I called you from outside the Rat after my final exam. Even though I had deleted your number off my phone, I couldn't rinse it from my memory. You picked up and I called you a dyke again, then a whore. You hung up.

A street kid stole the phone out my pocket before I felt like calling to say sorry.

XI

It's two months since I last saw you. I'm off Settler's Way today, on Brighton Pier. I'm trying to catch some shad. It's three o'clock and the beach is still full. It's about twenty-eight degrees, and the water is swollen with the easterly.

I've been here three hours and caught nothing. Earlier I spent three hours by the dolosse near town, and caught nothing there either. The lifeguards have had more luck than me: they've been pulling twitching bodies out the sea all day.

I've spent the summer at home. I've spent most of my nights at Pool City or the casino at the Boardwalk. I graduate in April. I don't plan to go back to Grahamstown until then, and even then I doubt I'll stay longer than I need to: ceremony in the morning, drinks at the Rat in the afternoon, safe in my own bed by midnight.

The gulls trace out circles overhead, looking for a good time to snatch at–

Shit. Is that you? God, I think it's you – with her – down on the beach. You have sunglasses and towels and a cooler box. I can't see your tattoo for your costume, modest and blue – but I'm certain it's you. Why are you here? You've put on weight. So have I.

I bring in my line. I pack my box of hooks and bait and lures and spare line and half-eaten ham sandwich and my half-jack of whiskey. I rush down the pier to the parking lot, keeping my head down. I can't bear to look at you for fear of turning to stone or clay or brine – what I'd turn to in your gaze, I can only imagine.

When I see that you too are in the parking lot, I freeze – ice it is, then. I have no car to hide behind, nowhere to stash my gear. So I turn back down the coast towards town. I don't know if you see me. I don't know if you say anything to me.

And so I traipse with my rod and my box and my heart in my gullet back down towards the dolosse, the concrete asterisks that break the idle ocean's waves. Placeholders for words unspoken. They stretch along the breakwater for miles.

I drop my gear and my sandals and climb the nearest ascender. I jump from one to the next. Up top I look over the breakers toward the ships and the deep blue of the sea beyond. The wind whips heavy with salt and spray.

I look back toward Brighton, over the green-topped dunes. To the left is the highway, the boundless N2, that pockmarked road back to Grahamstown. Transporters rumble past, burdened with cars from Uitenhage and elsewhere. Turning again, I stare toward town over the bay, the railway tracks somewhere, the cityscape and the Post Office building through the haze, its apartheid brown and blue visible even from here.

I sit down, my back placed in the arch of the dolos. The world is eggshell above and sea foam below. I could hear my heart if not for the ocean and the albatrosses and the trucks and the highway and the wind – the world, from here, an abundant [o] and [ʃ].

And then I hear your voice.

POSMAN

After a while you memorise the steps. You read the addresses and your calves just *know*, hey. They just know it's going to be a long morning.

These holiday homes on the steps don't get a lot of post. The German okes who buy them park in Frankfurt all year and only fly in when winter hits. Maar dis altyd mooi in die Kaap, né? Who even buys a house they don't live in? And houses like these, too. Most okes don't see them, so they don't even know what they're like. But let me tell you what: if I had one of these, on the beach? Jirre. I wouldn't leave.

But, ja, anyway – most of these places don't get a lot of post. Some municipal stuff, some late Christmas cards that'll sit in their boxes until next December. Sometimes I get these double-sealed envelopes met logos van strange banks al oor geskryf. Most of these okes dodge tax, hey. They have to. No one has that much money.

Some of the okes at the depot are jealous of me. They all say, "Piet, all you have to do is walk around the larney houses by the beach all day." But most of them don't know Clifton, hey. They don't know how many stairs there are. Jirre fok, all those stairs. Next time you go to Clifton 3rd, count the number of houses you pass on the stairs down. Ja, and that's my … that's my … what's the word? Jurisdiction. My *route*. They would die in a day if they had my job. And like, none – *none* of these houses have driveways. No paths. All of these houses are on the steps, going down the cliff. No other way in.

No, you have to chain your bike to the rails on the side of Victoria Road – ja, chain it with a combination lock because the skollies will take it quick-quick, even a Post Office bike, hey, they've got no skaam –

then take the stairs down. Ja, the stairs. Fifty down, fifty up, a hundred down, hundred up. Have you ever been to St James beach? Ja, just like that, but you can't see it from the road. You wonder how these okes get the shopping in, hey. Maids, probably.

And all these steps have these larney names. Dove Steps. Heron Steps. Arcadia. But they don't have signs and they don't have maps. No bru, go look on Google. They don't show the names. Rich okes don't want people to know how to get around their little paradise. So it took me a while to memorise, but now no one knows Clifton like I do.

So, like I was saying, every morning I get the post from the depot and I look at the addresses and I work out the route with the least steps. I don't need to run up paths I don't need to. So I look at the addresses – you know, I go down here, turn there, whatever – and then I have it worked out and I can get it done blitsvinnig. But not because I'm lazy, nee man. You should check these calves. I trialled for Vasco back in the day. Could be in the PSL. Making lekker bank, hey. But, you know, weak knees.

So most days I ride from Sea Point up to Kloof Road, right at the top, then carry my bike down Arcadia Steps to Victoria Road. Then I chain the bike and go back up Clifton Steps, back up to Kloof, then back down again. Then I ride down Victoria to the car park by Clifton 3rd, and I chain the bike and tune the carguard to check it, then I go down. I should count how many roads and steps there are between Clifton 1st and 4th, but I couldn't tell you now, not honestly. There are dozens, thousands. There's all this bush and dead-ends and the steps are so narrow and steep and, jirre, when it rains you're all slipping down the broken stones and all that sand gets clogged under your shoes.

But worse in the summer: it's hot, hey. And there are tourists everywhere lost on the steps trying to find the beach, and you're dodging them and they're always looking for directions, and I just want to say,

"The beach is in that direction. It's down the hill. The road is up the hill. Beach down. Road up. It's easy." But the worst is there's no wind and, jirre, it stinks. All the kelp and the sout and the piss from the toilets, and it's all just rotting there in the sun. All these miggies buzzing around, too. So you *sweat*, hey. And the Post Office asked us to stop wearing shorts now, so your balls get all sweaty and dit skaaf, hey. Dit skaaf. But that's work, hey. And it's a paycheck. And sometimes on an easy day, you can hide. Take a minute. See how the larnies live. Listen to the ocean and check the rocks and the okes selling lollies down at the beach. But those okes, hey. You know how their song goes? *A lolly to make a dolly jolly?* One oke now goes, *A sucker for a motherfucker!* It's a bit much.

But check: there's been this ou ballie around, and he's been throwing my system out. I'd tell you his name, but you never know who knows who, right? Anyway, he's at the bottom of these steps near 4th beach, right at the bottom of the promenade by the rocks and the sand, where the moffies pitch up on their yachts and lie out in their Speedos. And for the past few months, maybe, this oke's been getting post every day. Every single day, I swear. And he's way out the way. Like, going down to 4th from 3rd is OK every once in a while, but every day? It's an extra half hour at least. And that's if there are no moffie Fransmanne asking me for directions.

And this oke – this ballie – now, I don't judge, but this guy might be a moffie. He's got this big house – and I mean big. Big, big, *big*, all out in the open – I mean, with a wall around it, but you can see it all as you walk down the stairs behind. I didn't know you could just have just walls of glass. I mean, you see a lot of these things in Clifton and Sea Point, but jissis, this oke just has glass everywhere. I don't know how it survives the storms we have. Must be bulletproof – and he'd need it with all the stuff he keeps in there. Paintings an' sculptures an' these huge speakers. You couldn't even fit them in your car boot, so what's the point.

But ja, that's not why I think he's a moffie – I mean, ja, it's easier to be rich without a wife! But no man – like, every day, when I come down the stairs, he's on his roof and he's fokken kaal, man. Naked. Sunbathing even when the sun isn't even out. And he's a wit ou, but he is *bruin*. Skin like an old sofa. And his piel. *Jis* – I'm not a moffie so I don't stare, but you can't help seeing it – his piel is like a snail. Like a *big* snail, I swear, all curled up. And you don't want a burn on your piel. And I should know, bru: I once spilled tea on my lap at the depot, and I had to wrap toilet paper round my dick for a week. But this ballie just lies there, doesn't matter what time. Balls must be leather. Ja, I mean, sometimes I'd think he was dead if I didn't come down some days and his hairy fokken gat wasn't all out in the open. You'd wish you were blind, man.

But here's the thing. It just happened that, all of a sudden, he's out there, and he's getting all this post. And I'd remember if I'd ever had to deliver to this house before because, shit, I'd know if I saw this fat ou ballie trying to lure in okes with his balls. But he was just getting these dik handfuls of post every day. And shit from every which country! Nigeria, Germany, sommige small Italian place, San … San Marino, Colombia, Brasilië. And they were these dik padded envelopes, too, all computerised and double-sealed, and all like, you know, CONFIDENTIAL and DO NOT BEND. Serious shit, but you know, *weird* kak. But also, like, important. And these okes were just sending it to him, to Cape Town, through the regular regte ou Post Office. And we've had *strikes*, man. Strikes all the time. And these important okes are just getting stuff, you know, handled by who knows who, hey. I mean, there's no security, really. Anyone could open his post on the way to him and he wouldn't know. I mean, ja, I opened one or two – I mean, who wouldn't – and ja, they were just financial statements – I can't read fokken Duitse – but you know. If it fell into the wrong hands, I'm guessing this oke could lose a lot of cash. I mean, ja, this oke had cash. But I mean *cash*. Couldn't count the noughts.

So, after a while, I was wondering if he'd notice me, hey. Or if he'd get, like, suspicious. I ripped open one envelope and put it through the little letterbox in his wall one day – I was hoping he'd say something, but he didn't. So some days I'd whistle and pretend to stop at a neighbour and say, "O, dis die posman!" to see if he'd cover up his vuil ou piel. But he wouldn't move. He wouldn't even, you know, budge. No skaam.

So I just got on with it. I wouldn't say I looked forward to seeing this ballie, but anything seems normal when it becomes part of your routine, you know. I even took a pic of him on my phone and sent it to the boys at the depot, because they thought I was joking, hey. Now they think I'm a regte moffie. But, you know. They wouldn't believe me, so that's what you get.

But here's the thing I still can't get my head around. I was sick on Friday, so I just stayed at home and watched the cricket. First shift I missed in a couple years. And I felt *naar*, man. I didn't eat for a couple days, then on Sunday I ate three footlong Russians and just dossed. Jis, and I felt good on Monday, hey. Maybe I just needed the rest. I don't know. Anyway, so I parked my bike and I did all the deliveries on 3rd and 2nd side, and it was nice and cool, so I almost, ja, I almost jogged over to 4th side. And there were a couple stops on the promenade and I bought a granadilla lolly and ja, took it a bit easy – I deserved it, you know. Checked out all the cherries on the beach and the boats and everything. And at the end, I was expecting to see my ou ballie, but he wasn't there. His chair was gone and I could see all the windows and doors were closed. On the way down I was checking all through the glass, and I still couldn't see him. And it was strange, hey. This house

I wouldn't have noticed a few weeks ago, and now I'm staring into it, checking my hardest for this oke. And I had his post ready in my hand and I was going through it, to if there was anything strange, but there wasn't – just the same old padded envelopes and kak, in who knows how many languages. And so I just got ready to put them all in the letterbox, but when I got there, I saw he hadn't collected his post for a few days. It was all sticking out the flap like cigarettes. So I try to fit today's post into the box, but all these okes have small letterboxes. Then I reckon, maybe I could just throw it over the wall, but then what happens if it blows into the pool?

So I ring the doorbell, and wait for someone to answer. I wonder what this oke's voice will sound like, if he'll sound like all the other moffies, or if he'll be like a regte *man*, you know. But then I realise, you know, shit, if he sees me at the door and I'm sucking on my lolly, he might think I'm a moffie too and take me in. So I throw the lolly into the bush and ring the doorbell again. But no one comes. And I think, shit, I threw away that lolly for nothing.

But I think, well, I may as well try make sure this oke's post is safe, I want to go the extra mile – you know, Post Office: *We Deliver, Whatever It Takes* – so I take all the envelopes I can reach out of the letterbox and put them in with the rest of his post in my bag. I check the path to my left and my right, then I use the letterbox as a, you know, 'n vastrapplekkie, and I hoist myself up to look over the wall. Some of these okes plant rusty spikes in the ground to stop people from coming in, and I can't blame them for doing it, but jis, it must sting if you land on them. So I check and I see nothing. No dog, no people. There's a little light above the front door that I reckoned would flash if the alarm was on, but it wasn't flashing so I thought, OK, whatever. So I just jumped over the wall – easy, man, couldn't have been two metres – and went to leave the post by the door.

Maar, jirre, I couldn't have taken two steps before this fokken alarm went off. But it's not like any alarm I've ever heard. Not like a *wee-woo-wee-woo* kind of shit, but like a fokken air raid siren, like you're about to get bombed. Fokken *hard*, man. And so I just sommer drop the post on the lawn and I can see it already blowing toward the pool, but I don't care, there's this fokken siren going off, and I run back toward the wall and I put my foot on the letterbox and I jump back up. But I lose my grip and I fall, I fokken *fall*, man, head-first, and I cut my hand to shreds on the steps. Jirre, dit het gesteek. And it's bleeding and I'm just lying on the steps and this siren is going *neyerrr-neyerrr* so loud that all the moffies have probably stopped kissing each other and I just think, jissis, I'm going to look suspicious as all hell out here. So I stand and I brush myself off, and it's just my hands that are cut, so I fokken search in the bush for my lolly and I find it, and it's all vuil and sandy, but I wipe it off and carry it in my hand so no one will see the blood.

And I hardloop. I *run*, man, shit, up the steps, two at a time, and I just pray I don't see anyone. And I get to the corner of the ou ballie's steps and the 4th Beach promenade, and I can see people are looking around trying to work out where this alarm is coming from, and I just walk by, trying to look around, trying to look all casual, you know, and – I can't believe this – but I was licking that fokken granadilla lolly. It tasted like shit, but I just needed to look like I'm just doing my job. And I *am* just doing my job, I just got, you know, a little sidetracked. So I walk maybe a hundred metres and this siren is still like fokken *hard*, man, and I see these okes running down the promenade toward me, three of them, white guys, huge, all dressed in black with like shoulder pads and fokken army armour and everything on them. Like armed response okes, but not like your normal ADT guys. These guys were something else, carrying these huge fokken guns like you'd see some PAGAD gangster carry on the way to kill a drug dealer or something.

And in a couple seconds they were surrounding me and I just thought, no fuck, that's me, I'm dead, I've lost my job, I'm going to jail, they probably have cameras, *he* probably has cameras, and now they're going to catch me and I'm dead. And I'm beginning to, you know, prepare myself up to be arrested just so that these okes don't kill me on Clifton promenade, and they just look at me and say:

Hey, sir, have you seen anyone suspicious run by?

And I fokken lick my lolly and I say: Nee, meneer, but there's some alarm going on down there that you should check out.

And they say thank you, and they run off toward the ou ballie's house. And I just go, you know, jirre, and I put foot all the way back to Victoria Road, and I get my bike and go back to the depot and clock out and go buy a couple quarts of Hunter's. And I go home and it's too early to go to bed but that's all I want to do. So I map these quarts and I watch TV and, ja, just try to think about other things, hey.

I went to bed early but I just couldn't sleep. It was just so fucked up. My heart was beating like … like you know when you put your takkies in a washing machine? Like that. And even though those wit ous left me alone, I was thinking they probably had cameras in the house and they'd know it was me sooner or later and I'd be called in the next morning first thing and I'd be fired.

And, you know what, the next morning I come into the depot and the larney calls me into his office. And he looks me up and down and smiles all skeef and says: We're taking you off the Clifton route. And you can give us back your satchel.

And I thought, fuck man. All my nightmares. And I'm like, so you're firing me? And he looks at me double skeef and laughs. He tunes me: Ja, no, we got some word from an armed response company that you directed them toward an alarm and when they got there, there was some oke who had just broken in to some rich oke's house.

And I just gulped and thought, jirre fok.

And the larney just said, ja, no, they arrested this guy and it turned out he was wanted for break-ins all over the place, so it was a big catch and they were impressed with you. And he smiles and hands me a big padded envelope with my name all typed on it and says that I'm being promoted to a desk job – at the depot, nog al. Almost double the salary, nice hours. Said I can probably get my own little flat now, but what does he know – I already have a nice place and I'm fucked if I'm moving. But anyway, I was just shaking my head while he was saying his congratulations. And he said that I could go home for the afternoon and that they've already got someone new for my route. I asked who it was, and he said it was some new cherry they brought down from Mill Street side. So I just said cheers and thanks and went to the bottle store and bought some more quarts of Hunter's and sat down on the couch. I tried watching the cricket, but that was done by 2 o'clock. I didn't even finish my cider. I gave up trying to figure it out. I just dossed all afternoon.

But it's a funny thing, hey, the way these things happen. I saw the stukkie who's supposed to be taking the route this morning. She's a fat old thing, hey. I don't know much, hey, but I know one thing for sure: she'll get pretty skraal pretty quickly.

PONTA DO OURO

"Let's hope being a bastard skips a generation."

Mum folds her glasses and puts them next to her tea.

"Your dad's grandfather was a bastard too, or so your gran told me. Always at the pub, smoking in the house, hitting his kids."

I sit up. "Dad's never hit me though," I say. "And he doesn't smoke."

"Doesn't he? I've heard different," Mum says. "You see, that's the thing. You think he's one thing and he's really another, like–"

"Wait," I interrupt. "Dad smokes?"

"Apparently." Mum sips her tea. "Quinton said he saw him having a cigarette at the George the other day."

"But he hates cigarettes."

"Apparently not." Mum drains her cup. "He's a bastard, son."

"Right," I say. I flick the kettle on again and pick out another pair of teabags: our almost-hourly ritual.

"And then this," she says, handing me a sheaf of papers. "Take a look."

It's a divorce summons, faxed to her earlier today – 19 December, her birthday.

"Great present," she says. "'Irreconcilable differences'. Yeah, right. He's got someone. I know it."

He does. But she doesn't actually know it.

It's been six months since my dad moved out. It would have been longer if it didn't take him leaving and returning a few times before he found the courage or the motivation or the desperation – whichever it was – to stay away.

Either way, it had shocked me. I'd always thought my parents had a good marriage. At the very least, I thought they were decent foils: him, the dyslexic breadwinner; her, the librarian in Avoca Hills. But I found these things are rarely perfect. About a year ago, he stormed into the house after work and told my mum he wanted to be single. No further explanation. He took his clothes and his surfboards and left that evening.

Mum didn't take it too well. I moved back to Durban North from Glenwood for a week to see to her. My dad came back the day I was supposed to leave, so I decided to stay a little longer. Dad was out again within a couple days, and then back on his knees. Of course she forgave him.

This went on for a while until he signed a lease for a flat in Glenashley. I stopped going to lectures and took up drinking the beer he left behind in the fridge instead. Eventually I stopped paying rent on my flat and relocated permanently to north of the uMgeni again, to the house I grew up in on Lonsdale Drive.

I avoid him now. It's easy for the most part: he's either working in East London or stalking the pubs in uMhlanga village. Sometimes he insists I meet him for lunch at the mall in La Lucia, where I eat a wrap and chips and try to keep the conversation on the football. Other times I catch him after rugby matches at King's Park, where he's braaiing with his friends and their wives and daughters. Usually I pretend I've had too much to drink and that Yev is driving me home, just so that I don't have to drive him home myself. I'm still not used to seeing him stumble into Glenashley Heights, rather than the bedroom where he slept for the last nineteen years of my life.

Not that I think he stays there full-time. Soon after he moved out, he sent me an SMS that very obviously wasn't supposed to go to me. He didn't realise. I still need to tell Mum.

I'm sure I will, one day.

"Bastard," I say, trying to dispel the thought.

Mum takes our mugs to the sink and submerges them. She begins to sob. I get up and put my arms around her. Her hands soak through the back of my shirt.

We're supposed to go to Mozambique in a few days. I'm not sure if we will still. Mum says she has to get litigation started, and stays on the phone all afternoon. I start on a six-pack of lager.

She had wanted us to go away for Christmas, to spend time together that wasn't overshadowed by my father's presence – or maybe the lack thereof. She wanted to go to a place that she'd been to with her friends when she was much younger, a place she said where the world couldn't reach us. In her mind, a land of cheap rum, seafood and sunburn. A place called Ponta do Ouro, just over the border in Mozambique.

My friend Alex had told me Ponta was a shithole – too full of Afrikaners – and that we should head further north, to Tofo.

"Well, Alex is ignorant," Mum had said. "She's too bloody used to uMhlanga. The beach is clean in Ponta. No sewerage, no Indian wifeys drowning in their saris. Clean. Peaceful."

I didn't particularly want to go, but when Mum came up with the idea, it was the first time I had seen her excited since my dad left. Which was worth encouraging. So we booked a couple of nights at a place called Villa do Sol. It had looked all right online: wooden buildings, cane furniture with scratchy varnish, palm trees – the sort of coastal kitsch mothers take to.

The next couple days don't go so well. Mum holes herself up in her room with self-help books and hot toddies, coming outside only to go to Mass. I bring her meals – cheese toasties and takeout from Nando's – and mugs of tea. The dishes pile up. I go through a case of beer. My dad's sisters keep phoning us. I unplug the phone.

And so I settle in for a drunken Christmas, watching football. (Arsenal loses, twice.) I buy a large trifle from Woolworths and douse it with brandy. It doesn't last long in the fridge.

On the day before Christmas Eve I take my splitting head to the Pauline Sisters in Overport to buy Mum a present. I settle on a small statue of Our Lady crying and cradling the baby Jesus. The nun at the shop says it represents both Our Lady's joy at the birth of the Lord, and her pain for her son's eventual death. I say that Our Lady didn't know her son would end up being crucified when he was born. The nun says I'm missing the point.

When I get home, I ask Mum what she wants for Christmas lunch.

"Why?" she asks, sitting up in bed.

"So I can go to the shops and get a ham or something," I say.

"But we're going to Mozambique tomorrow."

"Are we?" I ask. "You don't seem like you're up for a trip."

"Nonsense," she protests, stuffing a tissue into her dressing-gown pocket. "I wouldn't miss it for anything."

I try to dissuade her, admittedly more for my comfort than hers. She won't have it. She gets out of bed and starts rifling through her cupboard.

"Get packing," she says. "You'll need sunblock and Tabard. I've got our passports. Oh, and start taking these." She tosses me a medicine container. Malaria pills.

"I'll be ready in the morning," she says.

She slams her door. I go and pack.

"Red sky in the morning!" Mum chimes.

"Shepherd's warning," I murmur. I'm hungover. My own fault.

We pack the old Land Rover with our bags and head north. I feel dreary, but on the road I begin to feel better. There's something life-affirming about driving north, past Ballito, Mtunzini, Kwambonambi – I wonder what it is? Perhaps it's the exoticism, the feeling of traveling off a national road, deeper into the cane fields, away from signposts to Gauteng, toward places with increasingly polysyllabic names.

Through KwaZulu, the world gets greener, the potholes more difficult to navigate. Buses don't run past here too regularly, not even in holiday season. So people line the road, up past Mtubatuba and Hluhluwe, looking for a spare seat in a kombi or between the kids in a family sedan. Hitchhikers hold up cardboard signs scrawled with the abbreviated names of their desired destinations: "RB" for Richard's Bay, "UL" for Ulundi. Closer to the border they hold up R20 and R50 notes. Kindness is easier to find when it's remunerated up-front.

I pass them all by. "You can never trust hitchhikers, not even the ones with babies," Mum says. "That's what they do, you know. They pretend they're rushing to get home and the next minute, they have a gun to your head."

Getting to the border takes longer than I thought it would. Traffic sits stagnant along the only road through Kosi Bay. Black families fill the pavements with packets of chips and old suitcases. White families pour in with boats and four-wheelers on trailers, clogging up the petrol stations.

Eventually we find ourselves at the back of a twenty-car queue to the border post. We get out and shuffle to the immigration office. We only have to wait half an hour.

"Purpose of visit?" the official asks us.

"Holiday," I say.

Stamp. "Welcome to Mozambique."

A guard gives our car a cursory look over before we cross the border.

We go from tar to dirt road, from dirt to sand. A vague path here and there, a sign that warns about unexploded landmines lurking somewhere off-course – but what course?

Car hooters are indispensable here. Hoot every minute. Hoot before you traverse a hill, in case there's someone trying to do the same from the other side. Hoot before you take a blind bend. Hoot at the GP-plated car tossing hand-crushed cans of Castle out their sunroof.

"Smell the ocean," Mum says, rolling down her window.

"Smells the same as it does at home," I say.

"Stop being so negative," she says. "Look, it's beautiful!" She's right. It is: the pearlescent sand, the unsmogged sky. "We're going to have such a wonderful time out here, just you and me. A peaceful time. Somewhere the world can't reach us."

A dune bike speeds past us just as I negotiate a hill. I hoot.

"Looks like the world will reach us just fine," I say.

"You're just like your bloody father sometimes," she snaps.

I stop the car. We sit in silence for a while, staring at the dunes. Sand blows against the windscreen in waves.

"I'm sorry," she says, eventually.

I start the car again. We go on.

ೞ

Soon the coast turns leafy. We see settlements, huts, houses. Wooden stalls by the roadside sell green mangos, jars of peri-peri, and rum in plastic bottles: the essentials. The palms grow taller, the paths better-trodden.

A sign emerges in the distance. Mum sits up. "That wasn't there last time I was here," she says.

It's for a night club: "CARLITO'S – THE BEST JOL IN PONTA".

"The best jol?" I ask. "Don't they speak Portuguese here?"

I slow down. I crane my neck to peer inside. Scores of sunglassed teenagers sit at picnic tables under canopies of palm fronds. Loud music spills out of unseen speakers.

"Grim," I say.

"Oh well," she says, "let's hope it hasn't all changed."

Closer to town, the sudden stench of petrol. Mum's nose wrinkles as we enter. South African plates adorn every car. Insipidly-named bars – Casa de Praia, Angelo's Shack – open up on to the main road. A Bulls rugby flag flies over one restaurant. A market lines one side: more mangos, more chilli, more rum. Clothing vendors sell MPLA shirts and slacks printed with the face of Nelson Mandela. Villagers watch us as they would a passing cloud.

"Jesus Christ, Mum."

"Don't blaspheme."

Then, a clearing. Across a small field, a harlequin strip of tourist accommodation, restaurants and shops. Our hotel is one of them: a clump of shit-brown chalets with green roofs. We enter the parking lot. Out front, there's a jungle gym infested with children. By the entrance to reception, a vervet monkey in a metre-high cage. A fanny-packed tourist has his camera pressed up close against the chicken-wire enclosure. The monkey swipes at the lens. The man jolts back.

We check in with a smiley man who carries our bags to the chalet. He kicks aside a broken flip-flop at the front door and dumps our bags inside. Out of breath, he asks us if we need any help with anything else. I ask him for a good place to eat prawns. Mum asks if there's a Catholic church nearby.

"Prawns, at Seamonga, just down the road," he says. "And church, just across there." He points to an egg-yolk yellow hall in the middle of the clearing.

"That's the church?" Mum asks.

"Yes, yes," he says.

"What time is Mass?" I ask.

"The priest, he usually comes at eight." He smiles. "But sometimes later. Just wait in the morning and he will come."

"Not the most reassuring," Mum says. "Anyway, thanks." Mum gives the smiley man R10 for his trouble. At this, I realise I never thought to exchange any money.

"It's OK," the smiley man says. "Everyone accepts rands here." How convenient, I think.

We decide to go the beach for the rest of the afternoon. I change into shorts and slather myself in sun lotion. Mum comes outside with towels, and we head to the shore. Mum smiles – this, at least, hasn't changed: white sand for miles, a sea pulling azure and mild-mannered; the bay's shallow curves and its freckling of boulders and rocks and pools.

We head to the bay, where most of the beachgoers loll about. We pass sunhatted men selling bags of prawns, bunched up like bananas. A gaggle of tweenage boys kick a rugby ball between them. It reminds me of someplace like home, cleared of its litter and black sand.

Mum stretches out her arms. "Glorious," she says.

We lay our towels out near the breakers. I kick off my sandals, lie down, and fall asleep. When Mum prods me awake some time later, I'm covered in sand.

"Get us a drink, would you?" she chirps.

I mumble something, sundazed.

"A Coke would be nice," she says. "With some rum. When in Rome, you know."

I swipe off the crust of sand and stumble toward the bay. There's a hut on the sand there. They should sell drinks.

A chubby boy, maybe ten years old, plays with a pair of scrawny white brothers outside the hut. They're throwing each other around on the sand, laughing while they pile on top of each other. The smaller of the boys is taking the brunt of it, but he seems OK. The fat boy's dad comes out the bar, shouting his name – "Fifico! Fifico!" The boy waddles inside. I follow and see him sitting on the bar top, chatting to some tourists. It seems his dad owns the place.

"You've gotten so big!" they say.

"Sim! Beeg!" Fifico says.

"His mother is a good chef!" his dad bellows, shaking his own belly in his hands.

I order a Laurentina and a rum and Coke. Fifico heads back outside while his dad pours my drinks. I pay in rands.

"Gooood," Fifico's dad purrs as I head out. "We like rands."

The boys are roughhousing again. They yelp and try to tug each other's hair. Fifico trips the younger brother, then laughs and offers a hand up. But the boy thrashes out and pulls down Fifico's shorts. A man outside the bar points and jeers.

Fifico disappears into the waves, his shorts still around his ankles. His dad peeks out from the threshold holding a tray of drinks.

"What happened?" he shouts.

"That boy pulled your son's pants down," I say.

"Filho do puta." *Son of a bitch.* He puts down the tray, jumps out onto the sand and treads out into the breakers. He scoops up his sopping child and stomps back to the bar, glaring at the brothers over his son's heaving shoulders. The two disappear into the back room inside.

I sip my beer. I leave.

Dark snatches hold quicker than we expect. We leave the beach after only a couple of hours. Back at the chalet, I shower in our shared bathroom. When I come out, Mum's reading her phone. She bites on the insides of her cheek.

"Hey," I say, putting my arm around her, "What's the matter?"

"Nothing, pal," she says. She leans into my chest and takes off her glasses. "Your dad just messaged me."

"And what did he say?"

"Oh," she says, placing her phone face down on the bedside table. "Nothing. Just wishing us for Christmas."

"Anything else?"

"Nothing."

She twists her wedding ring around her finger. I think I know what she's thinking, but she won't say it.

We head out to Seamonga, the place the smiley man recommended for prawns. So we eat prawns, gigantic ones, ten or twenty each, drenched in butter and peri-peri. Mum tries to suck the gunk out of each prawn's head, leaving a pile of soiled serviettes on the table.

"The head's the best bit," she says. I disagree.

I want to mention Dad, ask where he might be spending Christmas, what he might be doing, who he'll spend it with. Mum knows as little as I do, probably.

Across the restaurant, a young family shares a pot of mussels. "They look happy," Mum says, "Just like we were when you were young."

When we go to bed, I can hear Mum crying through the wall.

"Merry Christmas, darling."

Mum walks into my room carrying mugs of tea. She puts one down on the bedside table.

She kisses me on the forehead. "Come through when you're ready," she says.

I rise and open the blinds. It's overcast and still. I rummage in my bag for Mum's gift and bring it into her room. She's checking her phone, flicking through messages.

I give her her gift. I gulp my tea.

She peels the wrapping paper back. "Oh!" she cries, "It's beautiful." She kisses me on the cheek. "Thank you, darling. I love you."

"You're welcome," I say. "I thought it might cheer you up a little."

"Oh, it does," she says. She offers me my gift, a notebook with gold-leafed pages. I have two almost exactly like it back in Durban. I thank her.

We sit on her bed for a while, sipping tea. This is not like last Christmas. This is not like any of our past Christmases, when we'd sit on the floor, looking through cards from distant family members ensconced somewhere in the Iberian peninsula. Not like the times we would swim in the pool during afternoon storms. Not like the times we would eat handfuls of chocolate coins, littering the floor with a flurry of foil.

Mum drains her mug. "I think we should think about Mass," she says. "It'll be eight soon." She goes to shower.

I lie on the bed and watch the mosquitoes circle the room. At some point, Dad tries to call me.

∽

Outside the church, the women chat in their pastel dresses. The men, rugged and skinny, shuffle around in crinkled chinos. Children play with toothpaste marbles on the verandah. The doors are locked, but no one seems to mind.

"Excuse me," Mum asks one of the men, "do you know when Mass starts?"

He shrugs and smiles. "Feliz Natal!" he says.

Mum smiles back. "I guess we'll wait," she says to me.

A procession of dirt bikes passes by. The air fills with the cough and chop of their engines. The churchgoers cluck their tongues.

But soon afterward, an old Hilux bounds over the hill and into the clearing. A tiny, balding priest climbs out. "Feliz Natal!" he calls.

"Feliz Natal!" the congregation cries. They stand, uncreasing their clothes with their hands. Father strides across the lot, fumbling in his pockets for his keys.

Within a minute we're inside. We sit on plastic chairs. There are no pews, no kneelers. The altar is pine, draped with a thinning white cloth. No statues. No stations. No saints. The locals fill the left bank of chairs, the one closest to the lectern. We sit at the back.

After a moment's reflection, Father leads the congregation in a hymn. I can't understand it, so I concentrate on him instead: his sandals, his greying temples, his vestments stained with specks of oil.

He raises his hand and makes the Sign of the Cross with limp fingers. "Em nome do Pai e do Filho e do Espírito Santo."

"Amen."

We follow the aerobics of Mass – the sitting, the restless standing, the hesitant genuflection. The first half hour passes in mutual unintelligibility, a game of mimicry between us and the congregation. The priest's words are slippery and spongy, twisting and falling over themselves. We respond in English, to the stares of the children. I follow the shape of the liturgy: Penitence, Kyrie, Gloria, Psalms. The priest reads from the Gospel of João, proclaiming the coming of the Christ child.

"Alleluia, Alleluia!" we profess.

After the readings, Father waves at me and my mum.

"You are understanding?" he asks. I look around to see who he is talking to. It can only be us.

"Yes," Mum says, sitting up straight. "We are, I think. I mean, Mass is the same everywhere, isn't it?"

"Yes, yes!" Father leans on his lectern. "I'm happy you are here," he says. "Even though this village is always full of tourists, we don't get many visitors in our church." He waves his hand over the rows of empty chairs in front of us. "So we like it when you come. Welcome."

"Well, thanks for having us," Mum says.

"Where are you from?" Father asks.

"Durban," I say.

"Ah, good!" he says. "I like it there. Big city!" He turns to the rest of the congregation and speaks. They wave to us. We wave back.

Father says a few words to the congregation, something in Portuguese. He speaks softly, like a grandfather talking to a child. Then he turns to us again, his eyes wide.

"Now," he says, "I think in Durban you would have a sermon now?"

"Yes, Father," Mum says. "Usually."

"Good," he says. "In our church here, we don't have so many sermons. I don't like them. We are equal in the house of God, so I say here that we must listen to each other. I try not to speak too much. I let everyone else talk about the readings, the Gospel, you see, what it means to us."

"That's nice," Mum says.

Father steps down from his lectern and raises his hands toward us. "And as you are our visitors this Christmas, I think you should speak to us," he says.

"What?"

"Sorry, my English is not so good," Father says. "I said I think you–"

"Oh no, Father," Mum says. "I understood you. I just don't know why you would want to listen to us."

"You are our visitors," he says. "And we want you to share with us." Some of the congregation at the back start to shift their seats toward us. Mothers put their children on their laps. This is not like any other Christmas.

"Now?" Mum asks.

Father steps away from his lectern. "Yes," he says, nodding vigorously. "Now is good. You can speak and I will translate."

Mum looks at me. She knows I won't speak. And so she stands, under the gaze of the church. She shifts around on her feet, rolling the starts of words in her mouth.

"Hi, everyone," she stutters. "I suppose–"

She catches her breath.

"I suppose Christmas to me is about God coming down to earth and being like one of us." She waits for the priest to translate. "And that's important, because that means God is a person and it means we can think of him as a person. He isn't this big man up in the sky. He was once one of us, you know, living a human life with all of its pain."

The priest translates. The congregation murmurs.

"But it's also about family," she continues. "Not only God's family, but our families. We should celebrate family on Christmas. It's about my family and spending time with them as God spent time with us on Earth. And for me it's important that we're all together, me and my son" – I wave – "and, until this year, my husband."

At this her shoulders drop.

Father hesitates. "He is dead?"

"Oh! Oh no," Mum quavers. "We have just" – she searches for the right word – "separated."

"I am sorry to hear that," he says.

"It's OK," Mum says, but then she collapses onto her chair. I reach for her hand. She pulls away and wails.

The locals edge their chairs back. The children shuffle on their mothers' laps, dropping marbles out their pockets. A couple land at my feet. I begin to pick them up, abandoning my hysterical mother to her tears.

Father speaks in Portuguese again. He tries to explain, I think. The congregation tuts sympathetically, I think.

I take the marbles over to the girl who dropped them.

"Go on," I say. "Take them." She doesn't move. I give them to her mother instead. She forces a smile.

I go back to my mother. I force my hand into her fist.

Father comes over and squats next to my mother. "Are you OK?" he asks. She says nothing.

"Yes, Father," I say. "I'm sure we'll be fine. Just carry on with Mass."

He places his hand on my mother's shoulder. She looks up at him.

"Thank you," he says to her. He walks back to the altar.

Mum sniffs and leans onto my shoulder.

"I'm sorry," she whispers at last.

"It's fine," I say.

Father raises the Eucharist.

"We'll be fine," Mum whispers. I'm not sure.

"Hosanna in excelsis."

Outside the church, out in the clearing, there is a flag. There is no wind.

STARS

He was shouting at me for the first time since I'd met him.

"You fucked me over, Nandi. For fuck's sake."

"I know," I said. "I know."

"No," he said. "You don't have a fucking clue. You don't know what you've done to me."

"I know what I've done," I said. And I had regretted it. It's why I had come back to Durban. It's why I was here, in a bar by the docks, at 3am on a Tuesday. Wednesday now, technically.

"OK," he said, leaning toward me. "Seeing as you know me so well, tell me: how the *fuck* do you expect me to come back from that?"

To be honest, I was hoping he would have worked that out for himself during all the hours he had spent crying into his phone, with me silent on the other end. I had no plan here. I thought if I came here, things would just fit back into place like he said they would.

I heard they played jazz here, but there were just white boys playing chillwave off a laptop. When I walked in, I saw him dancing with another woman, an Indian girl in shorts, and at once I wanted to go back to your flat to eat rotis from Johnny's and binge-watch *Adventure Time*. But I stuck around, drinking vodka and ice, then beer, biding time. Now there were Thai sailors coming in, in starched-white uniforms, ordering shots of cane, flipping through the pages of a karaoke menu. I could see men with hotpants and imiqhele jiving to old Mandoza songs on the adjacent dance floor. There, a woman in blonde topknots danced alone, her wide-eyed spaniel sitting leashed to a vacant stripper pole.

The thing that surprised me most was this coming out of everything that had built up inside of him, unseen, seemingly unprocessed over the months. All his begging, all his flattery evaporated. He had his finger in my chest. "You *bitch*. You think you can come here for one night – one fucking night, Nan – and try to talk me back into bed with you? You think you can undo things just like that?"

"Bitch?" I said, wiping his spittle from my cheek. "When did you even begin to talk like that? That's not like you."

He shook his head, a statue of sinew. "It's not like me? Bitch, you don't *know* me." In retrospect, he was right about that.

"Please don't call me a bitch."

"I'll stop calling you a bitch once you stop being a bitch, Nan. What do you even want from me?" I had no answer for him, because suddenly I didn't know what the answer to that question should be. I felt all the spaces in my head depressurise, as if I was in a plane descending; and I stood there for a moment, not hollow, not empty, but reshaped and solid and ringing, like a bell. I felt now would be a good time to go. I felt that I should speak. And so I opened my mouth.

But what came out weren't words, but sounds. There was a shift, and there was broken glass, and there was a man shouting, grasping his elbow, rushing for the door behind me. And a hand at my back, and my breath taken from me, and my face against a chest, my mouth open, sucking in sweat from a well-known shirt. And I felt pushing, and his hand on my breast for the first time in months, but not in the form of a caress: a fist.

I heard his sneakers retreating just as my body jarred against the parquet. Men cheered; my dress had ridden up. When I found my feet again, I saw him walking back across the dance floor, toward the music coming from another room.

One of the Thai men walked over to me, and tried to caress my hip. "Hey boo," he said, his English seemingly learned from American hip-hop. "Hey shortie, you know I'll treat you right." His nose was thick with pimples.

I pushed him away, then looked for the Black Label I had left by my feet. I found it knocked over, its insides foaming out.

ᔓ

I found you outside in the mist, speaking to a car guard in French, your scarf tied around your head like a Bedouin's. A man stood hunched between the two of you. One of your hands was on his shoulder; the other lit a joint rolled in coconut paper.

"God damn it," I said, rubbing my hip. "Some guy just pushed me in there."

You met my eyes and shrugged. "Oh, swak," you said, pushing tendrils of smoke out your mouth.

Swak? I could have spat on you. You nodded your head towards the hunched man. There was blood on the tarmac, dripping from between his fingers and off the back of his arm.

"Oh, shit." I recoiled. "Shame, did he fall?"

"Nah," you said, smirking. "A hooker bit him."

"A … *hooker*?"

"Ja."

"Like a prostitute, right? Not a rugby player?"

"Ja."

"Why?"

You shrugged. The car guard motioned you to pass him the joint. You obliged.

The man pulled his hand away from the elbow, to check the bleeding. All of the skin covering his right elbow had been ripped away. The joint poked through, like a small knob of butter.

"Must've been an angry hooker," I said.

"He'll probably need a shot," the car guard laughed, taking a pull. I thought he meant vodka until he mimed a syringe going into his arm, joint between his fingers. "He doesn't want tetanus." He said tetanus like *tet-ah-nos* – like a Frenchman would, I suppose.

I bent down to the man. He wore zirconia earrings with a polo shirt and cargo pants, his belly sticking out in between. He smelt of milk. "Hey man," I said. "What happened?"

He looked up at me and I recognised him. "Hey!" I said, grabbing him by the shoulder. "You're the poes who pushed me. You got me punched in there."

"It's not my fault that someone else punched you, sisi."

"Wait, Nan," you interjected. "Who punched you?"

"T punched me."

"Why?"

"Because this poes pushed me into him!"

"I didn't mean to!" the man said. "I had to run. I got bit."

"Ja, ja, by a hooker – I know." Behind us the car guard laughed like a hyena. "Why did she bite you, though?"

"I don't know." He shielded his face under his popped collar.

"I don't believe that."

"I just tried … ugh." I prepared for the worst. Some lurid description of public assault, of another man trying to have his way. Wandering hands, wondering words. He hacked some phlegm from his throat. "I tried … I tried to eat her chips." He sighed deeply and re-inspected his wound.

"What?"

"I was hungry."

Far behind me I could hear the echo of your laugh.

ပ

"Nan," you said. "I feel like I'm failing you. You're my sister. I need to protect you from these men."

You'd stolen a six-pack of tallboys from behind the bar, with a practiced leap and a shushing finger in the direction of the Thai sailors. We split the beers, three each, on our walk back to your flat on Victoria Embankment – or Margaret Mncadi, or whatever the municipality had renamed it.

"You really don't have to protect me."

"Yes, I do," you said, cracking a can open as punctuation. "You make bad decisions." You slurped like a man who did not fear being arrested for drinking in public.

"You know what," I said, pulling a ring tab, "I don't even care. I've made some bad decisions in my life, but it's just life, you know. That's what you're supposed to do when you're twenty-two. Move cities, party too much, hang out in dangerous parts of town."

You took a slug from your can. Your scarf was re-tied around your neck, where it should have been in the first place, especially on a night as cold as this. You grunted.

"Come on," you said. "Sometimes I wish you'd get a grip. *Oh dear, I dated an asshole for a long time, but it doesn't matter*" – you strained your voice and waved your arms, as if that was how I spoke – "but God damn it. T *punched* you. You spent a lot of money coming back down here, to chase after this guy – not to mention however much leave you've taken – when you could have done something productive with it."

I matched strides with you, sipping from my can. The beer was warm and tasted of grass. The road was wet with old rain. The park glowed orange and empty from the other side of the light railway tracks.

"That's easy for you to say," I offered, "when you've never been in a relationship. Me, I thrive on them. Can't live without someone in my arms." I dodged a puddle in the sidewalk. "And I just feel so adrift now. I feel like the past two years have been a lie, loving someone I didn't really know. I– I just don't know what to do with myself." I felt water welling up inside me.

"You need to watch less *Girls*," you snapped. "I swear. All you want is *meaning* from your life. *Direction*. You think that making mistakes will make you stronger in the end. Your life and your feelings aren't any more significant or different to anyone else's, you know."

"But I don't think I'm different," I said.

"Oh, but you fucking *do*. You think every relationship is some epic. You kiss a boy and you go all *Wuthering Heights* on him."

"I've never even read–"

"You know what I'm trying to say."

I turned away from you, looking at the boats lulling at their moors. A breeze carried the sound of alarms from somewhere near the wharf. "Look, sis," you said, "everyone thinks they're special in some way – and, you know what, they probably are. Everybody has one very specific, very specialised thing that they're probably the best at the world at."

"Like what?" I threw my empty can into the gutter and pulled my second from my handbag.

"I don't know. Like whistling a certain song, or judging the traffic on a certain part of the road so you can get home the quickest way. Or, like, cooking an egg just right for someone."

"That's depressing."

"It *isn't*." You were raising your voice. "That isn't a reason to get depressed. Not figuring out the reason you're on earth isn't a reason to be depressed. Not being able to fucking align yourself by your relationships isn't a reason either. Because even if you found that reason, it's probably not the reason all the dumb TV shows you and your girlfriends watch made you expect it to be."

I eyed you. "What's gotten into you?" I felt like every man I'd ever turned to was now turning on me.

"I'm trying to be your *brother*. To guide you."

"OK, great guide, then what the fuck is depressing for you?"

"Chemical imbalances," you said, crumpling your can in your hands.

I wanted to disagree with you, to tell you how wrong you were about everything – but I couldn't think of any reasons then, although they're obvious to me now.

"You know," I said, "I also came to see you. Not just him." I was breathing heavily, too drunk to be expending this much energy. I sat down in the forecourt of the Engen on the corner of Hermitage, almost at your flat. I expected you to shout at me, to pull me up, but you left me there and fetched chips and Fanta from the shop. The old attendants eyed us from behind the glass of their office. We sat on the curb, mute, trading gestures for words, silence for argument.

When we got to your flat, three floors up, overlooking the docklands, I lay on the blow-up mattress in your living room and tried to ignore your rustling in the kitchen. I had asked you to make me a sandwich, but after five minutes you came through and handed me a cup of cold Ricoffy instead. You motioned for me to gulp it down.

"Get up," you said. "We're going swimming."

I'm not sure why you decided to drive to Virginia, when there were six or seven better beaches more within the reach of a drunk driver in a senescent old Saab. I had offered to drive, but you refused. In your mind I was still sixteen, incapable of modulating a clutch. You were driving up back roads, avoiding phantom roadblocks, with your last tallboy between your thighs and your shirt discarded on the back seat.

The streets were tungsten and tangerine along the Embankment, past the restaurants and hotels, past their tablecloths and beds, their old deals and consummations. The canopies of Berea and Morningside towered over us. You mounted a curb on Essenwood, swearing, checking your blind spot for police. Relieved, you laughed and ran an amber, racing to the M4. I sucked on a mint that I'd found swimming among the change in my pocket. It tasted of rust. I broke through its shell with my teeth.

I remember how empty the roads were. You were playing Debussy through an aux cable, the treble of the piano distorting from a subwoofer in your boot. I rediscovered how you lifted your little finger when you changed a gear.

"Why are we doing this?" I asked. This seemed like a bad decision.

"I felt like swimming." You took a swig of beer. "You need to chill out, sis. Be more spontaneous."

We passed the country club, and the vleis and the river, the lagoon dancing yellow, cityscapes inverted on the stillest waters; the checkerboard windows of the apartment blocks; the asphalt lakes of the hypermarkets. We overtook trucks of roadworkers, in yellow outfits, setting up crosses of blinking lights and bee-stripe warnings on wooden poles. We waved at them. They didn't wave back.

I remember how I searched for even a shred of moonlight above us, through the open sunroof, through the clouds.

I remember there were no stars.

ᔓ

This was to wash off what had happened on that night; what had happened to this life.

I hadn't seen you naked since we were children – and even then I had found it unbearable. Then at least you were shameless and sinuous and beautiful. Now, here, you were all untextured flesh, all baby fat at thirty-one.

The wind blew from the south. I wrapped your scarf around my face and sat on the sand in the half-light. I watched you charge into the silver waves, yelping like a dog, squeegeeing the water off your face with every breaker you broke.

You yelled for me to come in.

I looked up and down the shore. I saw the Bluff curving crescent, the skyscrapers, an audience of ships. I peeled off my jacket and my dress, and flicked my shoes away. My feet sunk into the sand. My ears were full of air, my heart full of blood. I followed you, to join you in this, whatever it was. And we were there, in water, impenetrably black and light-spangled, like the people in movies and on TV were, in the kinds of places where people can wash away their problems, in re-baptism, with lovers, with friends. Where people feel the wash of youth and the great expanse of the universe opening up in symmetry before them, with all possibility, all past before them.

But all I felt was the cold, and all I heard were your drunken yells.

The breakers were pulling and the salt was stinging. I stumbled from the waves, shivering and sopping, scraping the water from me as fast as I could. I felt I might faint. I lay on the sand, spreading my clothes on top of me. I tried to grip the ground, clumping the sand through my fists, the lights spinning, the firmament falling to the earth, orbiting elliptical and ceaseless.

You shouted and I raised my neck. You were running out the water toward me, with this look in your eyes, this crazed look I knew well. I closed my eyes, preparing to shriek, to tell you to get off me, to wrestle you, to feel your awful body on me as you laughed and grabbed at my limbs.

But you fell to your knees instead, your body lolling and protracted and shimmering. You began to throw up onto the sand. You retched and spasmed and made unholy noises. I shouldn't have opened my eyes but I did, and saw you, all this supposed strength and wisdom and age, half-prostrate on the dunes, the city glowing around you.

When you were done, you looked at me, and I allowed myself to look back at you, at your damp lips, your watering eyes. I grabbed your boxers and motioned you to put them on. You apologised.

The black of the sky began to split from the sea, slivering silver and sudden over the crests of the waves. The ships reclaimed their shapes from the horizon. A plane took off from the airport behind us, heading north into a leaden sky. Further down the shore, fishermen arrived, setting up their bait boxes, lodging their rods in the sand, casting into the restless grey. To them, today was a new day.

I could hear you snoring over the static of the wind and the water. "Hey," I said, shaking your shoulder. "Wake up. I've got a flight to catch." You grunted and shifted and raised your head. Sand had crusted around your mouth and nostrils. I turned my head to escape the bile on your breath. You stood and gathered your clothes, then trudged back to the car. I followed, tracking sand and esters and fragments of things to say.

I drove you back home as the rain began to fall.

DAUGHTER

Interlocked, we slide between the cabinets.

Far from the clamour of the schoolchildren and the cleaners, you tell me of your father – his pumice hands, the surety of his step, the sovereign that hung from his neck.

Here, must gathers: the glass rings fingerprinted; the labels curling brown, telling of South-West Africa, Zaire, Rhodesia. This museum holds things, you said, that we shouldn't remember. Things not worth remembering. The decades have no hold on the amethyst, you said, nor the lavulite, the asbestos silified and radiant, gouged like a heart still beating from the earth.

You tell me of your father – his agate eyes, his yellowed teeth, dried kernels, scattered in a field somewhere. The wood booms under our steps. Ahead, a creature of bones hangs from the ceiling.

Let's leave this place, you said – this apothecary of days.

You lean to kiss me between the back of my ear and the top of my neck; in that place that doesn't have a name.

It's not too far, you said.

GALA DAY

Here, look through the glass, scratched and greased from years of old breath. Here is the morning light.

Here is the mouth of the oHlanga, where the reed beds stretch for miles. See how easily the world unfolds here, through the hill's cleft, along the eternal coil of the M4. Pass the old La Mercy Hotel and its pastel trim. See the mangroves on the river's edge. Find the cerise of the houses in the old forest.

We lived childhoods of routine. A bus taken in the soft beginnings of the day, from the shelter by the Post Office, the one bejewelled with gang graffiti, sheltered by the decades-old palms. For five years, we were the only two picked up here. You lived in a duplex on Marine Drive with your grandmother. You wove through the taxi rank on the way, buying chips from the vendors. Every morning we sat on the bench, hips touching, sharing packets of murkhoo, the mynahs hopping at our heels. There was the sea air, the women speaking in Zulu, the earphoned joggers in polyester, peeling up off the promenade. You spoke about the football, fidgeted on your phone. You smelt of Lacoste cologne: you were always freshly showered. The gel in your hair was never quite set.

ᔓ

Doubles!

I never properly understood thunee. I never understood how it worked – why you used only twenty-four cards of the deck, why you kept score with the sixes, why a nine was worth more than a king. I never understood why you swore so much when you played it on the bus with your friends, using a seat torn out of its frame and balanced between your laps as a table. I never understood the palm-slapping plastic, your biting your father's chain, your rage so early in the day.

I never understood why you never looked at the ocean as we traced it, why you never thought about what was there, over the sea's shallow curve. If you'd asked, I suppose I might've told you Madagascar, perhaps, or Mauritius, although that was more north – I could never be sure of the trajectory. Maybe Perth and its high-rises, where your uncle lived. Perhaps he looked out too, from the other side of the Indian Ocean, and we might have unknowingly met gazes, if only for a second. I wondered about what we might have seen if only our eyes could see far enough. I heard a kestrel would be able to read newsprint from two kilometres in the air, if it could read. These were things I might have told you.

Khanuck!

Some days you wouldn't play cards. You'd sit with me. These were good days, even though your friends would tease you. *Wha-kish, wha-kish*, they went, slapping their fingers together; you were whipped. You would laugh at them, and you'd laugh to yourself at the white boys at the front, taking off their shirts in sight of the girls in the summer – they used the heat as an excuse. You knew the minutia of the bus: the primary-school kids, sitting mute in check-collared shirts, the matrics comparing tans and sunburns. There you would sit, with your earphones in, resting your hand on my thigh as I looked out the window. I pointed at things you didn't have the patience for. I always told you the eastward view was better; you said you didn't mind particularly.

I remember these things. I remember this one day when your hand slipped between my legs, just where the bus turned off the highway onto the gravel road that led up to the back of the school through the cane fields. The rumble of the wheels on the stones made your fingers move so perfectly there. I held your hand there for as long as I dared, turning away from you, resting my head against the window. I knew if you noticed, you'd pull away. Later on, in class, I could have sworn I still felt you there.

You made my blood rich with your touch.

ᔕ

There is cane here still. There is cane to the ocean, as far as you can see over the hills to the north and the west. One might disappear here, in all this green and shimmer.

The school grounds were large, or so they seemed then. There were clusters of red-brick classrooms, honeycombed around red-earthed quads and circles of wood benches and black plastic dustbins – all under the canopies of the towering flat-leaves. They were the tallest things here. One day you pulled me onto the roof of the biology class. There was no vantage. The world was brick below and cloud above and field beyond.

You cared little about schoolwork. That was something else I never understood, how you convinced me to bunk class, to watch you and your friends play soccer between the hockey goals on the bottom fields, to sit on the overlooking hill under the trees, trying to finish my accounting homework as the wind threatened to blow my ledgers away.

Perhaps the truth was that I never needed convincing. There were days when the glass radiated with dew, when the ball threw arcs of water as it spun, when it imprinted itself on your white shirt when you chested it down, marking you with the cause of your truancy to the teachers. There were days in winter when the grass went brown from drought and when the ground went to mud when it finally did rain, and your shoes would be caked and your socks stained.

You changed into something angry on the field, the same way you did when you played cards. You called everyone dickhead or ass-hole or tit. You did that even after that boy with the upturned collar punched you in the neck by the cricket nets one day. You'd called him a poes, you said, in jest. Later, when we on the bus home, you said you didn't know what to do. He was so much taller than you. I remember I started screaming at him, even though I was sure a teacher would hear us and catch us. It was unexpected, you said, because we all called each other names, even horrible things, and nobody seemed to mind it that much. I told you that sometimes what you say to people means more than you think it does. I told you that sometimes there's nothing truer than something said in jest.

Which, come to think of it, is something I sometimes think about when I think about the time you told me you loved me.

ᔓ

Every year the cane burns. It isn't good for the atmosphere, but it makes it easier to harvest. There are men and women who wear blue overalls and stalk through the rows of cane. They're still there. I know this because you can still see them from the road: chiselled and ragged and scything; beacons of labour embedded in the hills, far from my existence then or now.

One day, around September every year, you don't see them anymore. That's when you know the cane will burn. For days the air will fill with tuiles of ash, twisting in the breeze, settling in waves on freshly washed cars and bedsheets billowing on washing lines. If you were in a plane or a microlight, you might see the plumes scattered in the hills from Avoca to Stanger; ritual pyres creeping in the green, yielding to the sky.

I never saw the burning from the air, though. You had. You said it was magnificent, but it was nothing compared to being close to the flames. When the flames reached as far as the school, you and your friends would go into the fields through a broken gate by the nets. You'd try to find some cane that hadn't yet picked by the farmers.

You knew you'd be brought in and expelled if you were caught stealing from the cane fields, but I don't think you cared. It was worth that fibrous snap and twist, that sweet grain between your teeth, the smell of loam, the blackness that rubbed onto your hands and clothes. Each time you went, you came back bearing a stalk for each for us, your white Nikes soiled from the earth. We'd stretch out on the hill by the cricket nets. I would lie in your lap, clutching the cane while you used your knife to cut back the rind. I would bask in the smell of the smoke that had followed you back. I would taste the salt of the sweat on your lips as the school bell rang somewhere in the distance. Here was the completeness of the world.

❧

There was this day in the September before you died when you came back from the fields into the history classroom, the one painted with all the hieroglyphs by the matric artists. You sat down next to me and told me you'd found the most astonishing thing. I wondered how you could memorise my timetable and not yours. The teacher asked why you were there, his Pretoria arms bulging in their sleeves. You couldn't tell me what it was. There was a swimming gala the next day – you'd take me there then, you whispered, when the rest of the school was at the pool. The history teacher asked you why you weren't in your class. You said you were delivering a message from the maths teacher, smirking. You whispered to me that we could go straight from the bus to the fields. You were smiling. The history teacher told you to leave, pointing his arm of tattoo and sinew toward the glass door. You smiled at him. He told you he was watching you. You said you knew that.

The next day you said nothing while we waited for the bus. When it arrived, you sat at the window behind the Grade 10s and told me to come sit next to you. You plotted out our route on the glass of the window: from the bus stop, around the service quarters and the workshop, around the back of the science lab, under the balcony of the drama classroom, behind the row of bougainvillea, flowering pink, outlining a path down to the nets and the gate. I remember the air was hibiscus-sweet. The salt-chafed surfers in the back were shouting as we passed the lagoon. I couldn't remember what about – kitesurfers doing flips or a school of dolphins or something. That wasn't important. I remember feeling the hairs on my arm stand as you traced the flowers of mehndi my sister had scribbled on me the night before.

The girls in the back were slapping the talcum out of their swimming caps. It swirled in paisley patterns above us, making you cough. I heard the girls worrying about the weight they'd put on during the winter, about what the boys would think of them in their bathing costumes. I felt newly aware of the rolls of fat on my stomach, the way they moved and smudged together under my shirt when I coughed along with you. I wonder what you'd think of me if you ever saw me naked.

ഗ

I remember it was a Wednesday. Wednesdays were fasting days, and that day my mother had packed me a lunch that didn't have any meat in it. We'd been walking twenty minutes in the sun, through fields that hadn't yet been burned. You'd fashioned me a walking stick from a flat-leaf branch. We eventually found a clearing of sorts. Well-trodden earth and a bench. An empty Fanta bottle. There was a ditch running through the middle, a few metres deep – someplace to lie low if you were trapped by fire, I imagined. We sat on the edge of the ditch, our feet dangling into it. You'd brought a bottle of Energade. It was blue. I remember giggling at your stained tongue after you drank from it. I asked you how much further we needed to walk. You said it might be a while.

You told me about all these birds that we might see. I never knew a seventeen-year-old who knew about birds before. I still don't. You were like something you only saw in movies, like someone who couldn't possibly exist in the same world as me. You spoke about the petrels and the ospreys and the plovers and the lapwings and the sunbirds and the jacanas. You could have been making it up. You probably were. I didn't care. I still don't.

I asked you if you thought the teachers knew we were here. You said that there was no way no one could ever know we were here. I asked you about the farmers and the workers, what would happen to us if they found us here. You said that they'd kill us. I protested. You said you were joking, as if that made me feel better about it. I asked you how we would get back. You said the gala lasted all day, as if that were an answer.

I saw smoke rising over the hills. I remember the sky was opaline, the air heavy with salt. I asked you how much further we had to walk. It wasn't far, you said, just over the next hill. You pointed at a range of hills, all covered with cane. Just there, you said, pointing at them. I asked you if you were serious. You took a sip of Energade and handed me my stick.

I remember this. There were rows of brown and gold, restless – the world cremated, bones and cinder under the ibis's plaintive call. You pulled a stalk from the graying earth and cut its top with your knife. You offered it. I didn't want any, I said. You said it would give me energy.

Sweat gathered and dripped off your forehead. I wiped my mouth. There was this heat, this chiming in my ears. It must have been an hour later. I remember unbuttoning my collar, turning from you so you wouldn't see my chest. There was this compacting rustling inside me – my lungs felt like they were filling with ash.

When I woke, you were carrying me. Your steps were heavy. The sun was higher then. You had rebuttoned my shirt.

I told you to put me down, and you did, and I stood. The world came into focus: we were by a reed bed. This is what I wanted to show you, you said. I remember catching my breath. I couldn't find the air inside me to make into the words I wanted to say to you.

There were these barn swallows, hundreds of them, playing in the reeds. There was this twittering, this flittering in and out of the cane, this stripping of leaves and grain. This almighty swarm – they had perched on the reeds, flocked the attendant trees, filled the sky like the summertime ash. You said you'd read up about them. They were migrants, arriving to roost for the summer. They were uniformly tan and brown, their throats as red as if they'd been slit, swirling in patterns, these anxious constellations, occupying every interstice of the world. I told you that you were right: I had never seen anything like it.

You couldn't describe it, you said, so you had to show me. You couldn't describe the feelings it made you feel. You said you were giddy with air and freedom and other things you wished you had the words for. I never thought you were that sensitive, I said. You said you hadn't seen anything this beautiful before. You said you were frustrated that this had been hidden from you, from your view your entire life, things like these, these beautiful things. I told you that you hadn't been looking, if you thought that; that there were small beauties everywhere – I told you about the ocean and the dunes and the coastal forests, and the purples thrown by a clouded sunrise, the barreling seafoam; these were things I had already told you to look out for.

There was this brackish pond. I took off my shoes and rolled up my trousers so that I could cool my feet in it. I felt the mud between my toes. You took out your phone to take a picture of me, before this expanse of water. You said this was our own gala. You couldn't stop smiling. You told me you never wanted to forget this.

ഗ

There was the wind and the birds and the fields. You and I spoke in ways I'd never speak now. The roughness of our words are now sanded out: the slanging umlauting, the crooning curling of our tongues. I wouldn't want to forget your words as we lay there, in that ditch, after I had broken my ankle.

But this was long ago. You told me these things that made me feel these things, but not in these exact words: that I was beautiful, like the vista of swallows; that you had never met anyone like me; that you were sorry you had brought me here and that I'd hurt myself, but you wanted to show me something that looked like how you felt about me. It was comfort to me. There was this throbbing in my leg – but I'm still not sure if mine were tears of pain.

You had called someone to come and help us, but you didn't know where we were exactly, and they didn't know where we were either. Who could be sure of where these gullies lay, or how many they were? I told you to leave me, but of course you never would. We had the remains of my lunch. There were hours of daylight still. There was the wind and the birds and the fields.

After – how long, I'm not sure – there was this rustling, this whipping, this *wha-kish* above us. There were these two men in overalls, unbuttoned and dangling around their waists. They had pangas hanging from their workbelts. They stood above the ditch, above us. The shorter man had cropped hair and sucked his lips. His face was covered with some kind of clay or sand or lotion, like a mask or a mismatched foundation. The taller man had a jaw like a set-square. He was sweating like you were.

You stared at the men. You were worried that they thought we were here to steal cane, like you said earlier. You said to them that I had hurt myself, that we just wanted to get back to school. The tall man sighed and said something. The short man clicked his tongue.

You were in conversation, but I couldn't understand it. You knew this. I still wonder about that. Their words washed over me. The one said ubani and the other said angazi. You protested something they said. You said you were telling the truth. The tall man clicked his tongue and took his panga off his belt. He cut off a piece of cane and threw it on top of us. He laughed. I began to cry – these were more knowable tears. I wriggled further into your embrace.

The tall man sniffed. He said something, I thought sympathetically. The short man said bandla. Bandla, he said, again, sniffing. Bandla, something like that. I saw his blade glint in the sun. The tall man came closer to the edge above us. He leaned over, his head blocking out the sun. Behind his shoulder, behind this shadow he'd become, I could see the smoke beginning to rise again. You kissed the back of my head. I felt the warmth of your breath. I saw a bird flit above, warbling and iridescent – I might have imagined it, I can't say. There were these waves of words, words I don't know if I didn't know or not, words that washed over me and filled me and every space within me. I remember closing my eyes, I don't know for how long.

You were scrabbling. You took hold of my wrist. You tried to yank me up, but I couldn't hold myself upright. The short man had jumped down. There was dust in my eyes. You told me something quickly, but I can't remember what it was. I fell again. There was this smell of carbon, like pencil shavings. The tall man was above me, clicking his tongue. Bandla, bandla, something like that. There was no energy for shouting.

The short man said simfukule, or something. I could look it up now, I suppose. Something to do with amandla, too – power, or force, or energy. I can't guess anymore. There was too much to remember. He kept on telling you to stay quiet.

I remember he bent down over me.

DIE BIBLIOTEEK VIR BLINDES

And do you know what kind of books they have for children? Jude, you would *not* believe it. Shame, let me tell you. When I walked in there, you know, I saw them and I thought, oh my goodness, what are *those*? They were all over the table, all blue and red – and pretty, you know. Bright. Little fluffy books – like cuddly toys – soft pages, all fat like stuffed handkerchiefs. All, what's-the-thing, like furry? Ja, ja – velvet. And there was this – you know braille, like those little dots? – all printed on plastic and stuck on the velvet. There were these captions in Afrikaans and in English, like "Find the toothbrush", and on the next page – I'm not kidding, Jude – there would be an *actual* toothbrush stuck there. And you'd turn the page and there it said, you know, "What is this?" all in English and Afrikaans and all in this braille, and you look over to the next page, and there's this real plastic comb superglued onto the velvet, with its prongs all broken. I swear to God, Jude, every second one was broken. How can a child know that *that's* a comb?

Ja, and a blind one nogal?

And I just thought, Jude – *shame*, you know? God bless, hey. I felt so bad. And there was this woman sitting there by the door on Thompson Street, when I went out. I didn't see her when I went in. And she was this blind lady, you know, a coloured lady, and she was looking over at, I don't know, nothing, I suppose, and she must have heard me try to sneak by her but all the floors were wooden – ja, you know how those old houses are – and she said, "Hello, hoe gaan dit?"

And I just froze. I just *froze*. And she said, "Have you had a look at our art exhibition?" and I almost laughed in her face.

Ja! Blind art! So I asked, you know, “Oh my goodness, art by blind people?” And she said ja, and I said, “How do they do art?” and she said – Jude, I swear she said: “Why don’t you go see?” Why don’t you go *see*, Jude! I swear.

No! I know! Then I did laugh, hey, and I think it was a joke, because she was laughing too, but you can never be too sure, hey?

So I thought, you know, let me have a look – hmm? Ja, another cappuccino, thaaank you – ja, so I just thought, let me have a look, hey. May as well. And I swear these blind people, God bless, they’d taken all these photographs and thrown some paint on some paper and gotten someone to frame them and put them up.

I know! They can’t even see it! How do you exhibit something you can’t see? The mind boggles, hey? But let me tell you, some of them were pretty good.

Ja, no, not just for a blind person either, you know. There was one girlie, some girlie, who could sort of see things, like the light and a few shapes en daai goete, and she had used a phone camera to take photos of plants and trees and, you know, they were pretty. I thought about buying one of them, you know, to support, but the blind woman at the front said they weren’t selling anything. I know – you’d imagine! And I had just thought I needed something to cover the wall in Silvia’s room out the back.

But anyway, I thought, you know, shame, I’d love to support them *somehow*. I felt bad just coming in and having a look at all their blind goete and leaving, even though I’ve only been walking by that library for so many years and never given a second thought –

No, you neither? But curiousity bit me, hey, and I was feeling bad, so I said to the girlie, “Well if you’re not going to sell me a picture, is there something else I could do?” Ja, ja, I was thinking donations, hey, maybe twenty rand or something. But do you know what she said?

"We don't accept donations!" Can you believe it, Jude? I mean, can you? No man, she said they get all their money from government.

Ja, so that's where our tax is going, hey. To the blind! Ja, ag–

Ja, ja, and all his wives, too!

So anyway, I said to her, "Well is there any other way to help?" and now I couldn't just leave because I've been talking to this blind girlie, and she said, "Oh you can volunteer," and I said, "How, re-arranging books for you?" – and I almost started laughing. I mean – no really, it's what I said. Ja, it was bad, hey. Shocking of me. But she said, no – get this – "No, you can record an audiobook for us. The students from the university do it, but we could always use more people." And my jaw just hit the *floor*.

Ja, ja, *ja!* You know I've always wanted to read audiobooks – ja! I *know!* And at first, I was – you know, um, what's-the-word – hesitating a bit, but I thought, you know, ever since Jan went, I haven't had much to do. And you know I used to do the classics on Radio Grahamstown before the "new management" took over. I haven't had much to do – oh, no thank you, we're OK for now, ja thanks – and I said to the girl, ja, you know, OK, I'll give it a go. And she said, "Oh lovely, come in Wednesday." And this was on Monday, you know, so I thought, OK great, I have something to look forward to. Because you know, all I do is sit around the house and read the *Reader's Digest* anyway.

Oh, but then! You know how the weather was on Wednesday? Ja, it was scorching! Thirty-five degrees? You're *kidding* me. Well, anyway, it was that hot, and the library didn't have aircon. The woman at the reception was fanning herself with one of those Japanese fans from the shop next to Checkers – you know the one? Oh no, she could see, the receptionist. Well, ja, I don't know? Can you do accounts in braille? But ja, all the people upstairs can see. I think they just keep all the blinds downstairs, to say hi or something. Ja, be the front or the face of it or whatever.

Ja, so, anyway, this receptionist called this other girlie, this other coloured girlie, and she was all smiles and chats and, you know, I thought this would be nice. So she takes me up the stairs and there are these little cubicles, maybe two or three, all with foam on the walls and lots of wires and technical goete all plugged into a laptop. And like a hi-fi, or something. Ja, ja, like the radio station, I guess.

Ja, no, not big, maybe as big as this booth. Ja, small, but so, *so* hot. I was already sweating.

So the girlie sits me down and tells me what to do and – ja, it was pretty simple. She does all the things on the computer and then she says she'll cut it together and edit it and so on. I signed this form – ja, I don't remember what it said –

Mm-hm, mm-hm. No, no, I'm fine for now.

Nice girlie, hey? She's always nice.

So, anyway, this girlie upstairs says she's going to start me off on something easy and she gives me a book of short stories. And it looked quite nice. A bit larney-looking, you know, but the cover was nice. It looked new. The colour of your top, actually. I asked her where they got the book and, get this, she said says they borrow books from, you know, the second-hand shop across the road. Ja, ja, where the woman who thought she was a man worked!

Can you *imagine?*

So she starts recording, and she closes the door and I just sit in there and start reading the story. And it was actually a nice story at first, actually. It was in Paris, and there were these two nice young African boys going around some galleries and the Eiffel Towers and looking at some paintings and talking and things. Ja, and there was some guff I didn't quite get, you know, but I was enjoying myself, and the reading all came back to me and the girlie brought me through some tea and it was, ja, nice. But hot, you know.

But ja, anyway, I'm reading and reading, maybe about ten pages, and getting to the end and then bam! There were the most disgusting sexual bits. Ja. *No* – between the African boys! Ja, ja! Can you imagine? And I thought at first I should stop reading, but I kept going for a few more sentences, but then I just couldn't anymore, Jude. I just couldn't.

It was vulgar. The most disgusting, perverted things. I was in shock, you know. I just felt my cheeks going red. Those perverts! You know? Who would write those things? And to put it in these stories? Who … ja! And the language! Ag, it was just awful. And so I stop and I say to the woman, you know, sorry, I can't read this, about these homosexuals, I'm a Christian and this is just vulgar. And she just looked at me and said, well, I'm sorry, this is the book you have to do! And I was *gob*smacked. Just gobsmacked! And I said, well, can't you give me another book? I thought it was reasonable, you know, and she said, no, you actually have to do the book you're given, there's like a system or something. Ja, a procedure.

And look, Jude, I get it. I guess the blinds need, you know, some *help* sometimes – ja, ja, we all do sometimes – but I told the girl, you know, no thanks. I'm not reading this filth out. I'm not going to let some blind pervert, you know, get off on my voice, you know? How is this appropriate for a woman like me?

But ja, that's what she said – "No, you have to do the book that's in front of you." Once you started something you had to finish, otherwise it messes things up. And I just said, you know, no! And she was nice in the beginning, but now she was getting angry. She said that I was so close to finishing and I was doing such a good job, and ja, I thought I was doing a good job, but then I said I'd be happy to read another one, and she said – do you know what she said, Jude? She said, "No, if you don't finish it it's a waste of my time." The nerve of that girl!

Ja, I know! And she thought she was so larney, bossing me around. Ja, ja, I should have known. No – young! Maybe thirty? Ish?

Anyway, you know, I just thought: typical. You want to do something good for someone and then they just take advantage of you, hey. Ja, it's a shame. I'd been sitting there for almost an hour in the heat and she was treating me like this and she thought it was her who was being, you know, inconvenienced when she's the one asking me to read filth like that. She thought it was all about *her*, hey.

No, I had no idea. No, all kinds of authors I'd never heard of.

Ja, so inconsiderate. So inconsiderate. So I just said, "Well no, thank you," and I got up and left. And the nerve of that girl! Do you know what she said then, Jude? Oh, you wouldn't believe it. She said, "Oh you're all the same, you people!" Ja, that's what she said: *you people*. And I said to her, "That's not a very nice thing to say," and she said, "Ja, that's all you people do. You say you want to help but you just come in and complain." And I just lost it, Jude, I just lost it. The nerve of that girl. I asked to speak to the manager and she said she was the manager. The nerve. And I just, you know, left.

Ja, I sent one to *Grocott's*. And I mean–

Look, Jude, I do what I can. You know, I don't do a lot, but I do enough. I think. You know, the church and the MySchool card. So I just wanted to help, and I thought I could have done a good job with my experience, and I was actually starting to get so excited about it, Jude, I really was. It was something I thought I could really do, you know! Something to keep me busy. But people like that just make you think, hey. What kind of country–

Ja, exactly. *Exactly*, Jude. I couldn't have said it better. You know, and they get volunteers – for blinds, nogal – and they just send them away like that? And when I walked out, the receptionist was just giving me the eye, you know. I think she heard our conversation. And I just felt like saying to her, you know, is it too much to ask you not to make me feel too uncomfortable while I'm trying to–

Ja, exactly! The nerve.

Anyway, I'll move on. Just disappointing, you know. Shame, at least it was better than your Wednesday, hey? I *swear*, I–

Oh? Ja – thanks, just the bill, please. Thaaanks.

I-HR FOTO

Wern came from the back in time to see her leave. At first he thought of chasing her into the damp heat outside, of striding down Mackeurtan Avenue, under the dappled shade of the mahoganies and the coral trees festering with mynah-chatter. He thought of pinching the ends of a film canister between his index finger and thumb, before hurling it expertly at the back of her head.

But he reckoned there were professional obligations at stake. He stared at the paper bag on the counter. She had scrawled on it:

MACKEURTAN 1-HR FOTO • 5 MACKEURTAN AVE, DURBAN NORTH • 563 4433

NAME

MS S DE COSTA

DATE

7/10/2003, AM

ADDRESS

53 LANSDOWNE CRES
DURBAN NORTH

CONTACT NO

563 6501

INSTRUCTIONS

2 FILMS, 135
PROCESS + PRINT, MATTE, *please*

Her maiden name. His old address, opposite Northwood.

"Sorry, bra," Dees said, behind the glass counter at the shop's front. "Don't know why she'd come in here of all places."

Her handwriting hadn't changed.

"Not too surprising," Wern sighed. "Not as if there's anywhere else to get photos processed around here."

He shook the bag, the canisters clacking inside. He rolled the contents onto the counter. On the left, Reala ISO 100; Superia ISO 800 to the right.

"You know CNA's stopped taking film, hey," Wern said. "All of 'em, they only print from disk now."

Dees was on his haunches, adjusting the cameras in the display cabinet below the till. "Ja, I heard," he said matter-of-factly. "Hope it brings more customers in."

Wern turned his back, palming the roll of Superia, judging its weight as he would a flat stone on a riverbank, then placing it upright on the counter. He found himself tracing the writing on the packet with his fingertips: the loop of her Os, the forward slant of her upstrokes, the flourishes between each letter.

Two years already, he thought.

He was about to say something to Dees – something off-hand, something casual to shake the feelings growing inside him – when a man with reflective sunglasses came in from the heat outside and asked Dees about buying a digital camera. Wern crumpled the paper bag in his hand, picked up the canisters of film, and went to the back room.

The air smelt of solvent and rot, from an old Tupperware of mango that Dees had left in a corner. The machines were dormant: Saturdays were slow business. Still, it suited Wern. He liked to take his time with things; to make sure every image was as perfect as it could be before it went out. Above his computer hung a corkboard covered in cobwebs of twine and post-its, instructions and checklists, the preferences of his regulars.

There were perks to Wern's breed of fastidiousness. On the computer, a panoptic catalogue of neighbourhood vice, curated during the hundreds of hours he spent on quality control. Self-portraits of technikon students, with their pale breasts and languid limbs and steeled faces. Hurried, overexposed snapshots of intimacy entrusted to him by strangers. The collections of teenage friends, of friends' daughters, brightly bikinied under beachfront umbrellas. There were poolside photos from newlyweds, interspersed with their evening dates and couplings. The latter were his favourites, if he could allow himself to say he had any. He thought they told a story, something he could conduct, like music; something he could hang onto.

Wern kept these on a different hard drive to the one that held the photos of him and his ex-wife – of him submissive, of her lingeried and stripped, of them together, flushed and fine-focused. They were once pictures of pride, developed after hours, meticulously retouched, released of their blemishes, of their unevenness and – he hoped – of their ordinariness. Recently, though, he found them too refined. A kind of airbrushed nostalgia, for something that really never was. There was newer material to supplant her now, memories that felt realer to him. He thought about deleting the photos of her, burning the hard copies, those remembrances. Soon, he thought. Perhaps he owed it to her.

The faux-granite top on Wern's workbench was beginning to wear thin. On the shelves above it were envelopes and sequentially numbered pairs of stickers, seven reels of Sellotape, a tangle of lanyards and three trays of floppy disks, rainbow-coloured and smattered with the remains of sticky labels. The processor whirred behind him. He took a film extractor from the top drawer of the bench and pushed its tongue into the opening of each of the canisters, pulling the ends out. He affixed numbered stickers – 6076, 6077 – to each of them.

The lights flickered above.

He picked up the packet again, half-scrunched at his feet. Perhaps, he thought, he had missed some special instructions, some indication of her usual particularity, something that could cause her to complain should he get it wrong – but there was nothing. No list of specifications like those that accompanied the first exposures he ever processed for her, sixteen or seventeen years ago, in the makeshift darkroom of his old Westville flat. During the course of that evening, after he had spilled an indelible streak of fixer across his landlord's carpet, he came to know the reason that one day he would come to love her: her photos. Silhouettes of ibises against china-blue skies, portraits of children eating cheese sandwiches outside Garlicks, shots of hawkers on Smith Street – things no one had made beautiful for him before.

Wern rubbed his palms on his shirt. He thought about what these rolls might yield. He taped the Reala to a plastic card, lifted the lid of the processor and inserted the film. Soon the negatives would slither out. Soon he would know what she had given him to see. Until then, they, like all photographs, existed only in a Schrodinger's state; as expectations. That was the beauty of photography: how at first the pictures only really existed in your mind. And how, when the negatives arrived, you might find that the images didn't appear the way you had imagined them. Perhaps the focus was wrong, or the light was read incorrectly. Tricked by biology. Tricked by mechanics.

Before the canister is cut and the film is extracted and tracked across the sponges and through the chemicals, pulled by the actuators and the rollers into the darkness and the sulphates and the acetics and the fixers and the rinsers and the dryer, he thought, that's all the frames are: hopes, some finely calibrated, some spontaneous and little thought about, if at all, until they're held in the hand or against the light, and you can see, finally, yes, this is how I imagined it; or, no, this is wrong; this is totally wrong.

That's what's wrong with digital cameras, Wern thought: they're nothing like life.

A dull beep. The negatives were hanging out of the far side of the processor. Wern turned back, taking the flaccid strip, unclipping it from the card, and laying it down on his bench. With a guillotine he cut it into six equal lengths, then clipped each one to the top rim of an unlit light box. He consulted a lever-arch file on his desk before setting the processor for the second film, which he sent on its way.

He could hear the drone of the radio drifting in from the front, where Dees was still talking to the customer. The presenter was warning of thunderstorms. Wern shut the door and turned off the back room lights, coasting around the whining processor to switch on the light box. The bulb hesitated, then glowed, white and stark. On its front, the strips of negative, toned under casts of amber and black and blue, revealed their forms.

They'd been to the bird park, her and the girls. He read the strips in sequence, like a comic book. On the first two, Wern made out the inverted outlines of his daughters' faces – black, brace-straightened teeth, black eyes with glowing pupils, electric streaks of hair draping to their shoulders. In the middle, frames of toucans in wire cages, peacocks fanning their tails, ferns and delicious monsters; half a dozen blurs of life too fast to capture. There was a man in the final set of frames with the girls, embracing them. Wern couldn't tell who he was.

He felt nothing. That surprised him. He studied the film: no scratches, no streaks, no dust. He unclipped them and set them aside to scan and print. He thought about how he hadn't been to the bird park in years.

He should really make the effort, he thought.

A dull beep. He walked to the processor in the glare of the light box and carried the second length of film between his arms to the guillotine.

These images looked familiar, he thought. There were limbs against the unmistakable crease of sheets. There were heads thrown back, mouths ajar. There were breasts speckled with moles.

He didn't blink until the light had burned the shape of the six strips into his vision. When he closed his eyes, he saw the positives emerge; the colours and the forms popping into their right inversions; the tiny frames swelling and filling the inside of his mind, the tiny arms and legs and extremities expanding and swirling and leaking into each other.

He opened his eyes, imprisoning the images again in their strips. He heard the click of the air-conditioner as it oscillated. He licked the sweat off his lip.

Wern unclipped the negatives, and walked to his computer and the hulking scanner beside it. The monitor degaussed, and the room – and the corkboard with its string, and the machines with their slow blinking buttons, and the shelves of everything – glowed softly blue. Wern took a plastic frame and set the negatives inside them, clipping them into place by their sprockets. He loaded the frame into the scanner and clicked and cursored. From the pre-scans, fuzzy and inexact, he could already see her. These arms could have been his own, hirsute and browned only from the elbow down, gripping her throat. He could see the corners of a painting he had once bought, above a bed he had once slept in.

There was a curdling in his chest. He stood and walked to the door, turning the key gradually to muffle the sound of its locking. He could hear Dees talking on the phone, but he couldn't tell what about.

He went back to the scans, selecting and cropping and adjusting each one in haste, trying not to look too carefully, until what sat before him was a polyptych of flesh and frame and fluid. He sent them to the printer – 4x6, standard, matte, just as she ordered. It bellowed into life from the corner of the room.

As he sat there, alone, waiting for the prints to emerge, he undid his belt, reached into his briefs and found himself hard. The printer whined and began to flick out the prints. Wern sat in his chair, his face lit by the screen. He could hear Dees call for him, but he couldn't tell what for. He thought that he hadn't felt this alive, this bright and electric, since she had left. Perhaps he wouldn't ever feel like this again. A photo came on the screen of the man with his daughters. Wern let go of himself, and readjusted his seat. He saw that the man looked nothing like him. He imagined his once-wife again, under him, discovering her noises like he once did; the things the other man had already discovered that he hadn't; the new things she would learn from him; the things his daughters might learn from him, too; things like letting go, and adjusting to change. Wern resolved, right then, that he would shake the other man's hand if they ever met. He would act mature, reserved, professional. To show that he had grown.

That he had developed.

The whine and the whirr and the dull beeping aloud and aloud and again. Wern packed the prints into the envelope and slid the negatives into a plastic sheath. He fingered the handwriting on the envelope before he unlocked the door and handed it to Dees at the counter. "Don't tell me when she comes," he said. Dees nodded, and sipped from a small glass of Fanta.

And Dees wouldn't, twenty minutes later, when she arrived; when, after scanning the room and seeing the back door closed, she'd leave with the envelope in her handbag along with a receipt for fifty rand. She would sit in the car, hiding a smirk, certain of her triumph. Untrusting, she would flick through the photos, to find anything hidden, anything shuffled between the two sets of pictures – but they would be sorted immaculately, as ordered. She would hand the correct set of prints to her daughters, telling them to be careful not to get their ice cream on the pictures. And Wern, hearing cars pull out of the lot and back down onto Broadway, imagining which murmur of which engine belonged to her, would sit with an address book open in front of him, lit by the light of the subfolders on his monitor, hearing the drone and warble of the dial-up modem and the fax machine, echoing the world outside. He would hear the first thunder, the dull slam of Dees closing the windows, the electricity humming in his nerves.

And there he would click. He would scan and dial. And as the first storm of spring announced itself on the trees and the cars and the streets outside, Wern dispatched the photos she gave him to every person he knew, and to every person he knew she knew. All the secret moments, all those hidden places, flickering through the phone lines; private no more.

And, sitting alone and silent in his back room, Wern would hope, at that instant, to make her feel every bit as alive as he did.

APPRECIATION

Sister hoists herself up at the end of Communion, an iron crucifix swinging from a length of twine between her navy-cardiganed breasts. She interlaces her fingers around an old microphone and holds it close to her mouth, even though the power has been out in town all day.

We strain to hear her voice as it quavers. "There were ten students last month who volunteered to start shifts at the Sibusiswe Nutrition Centre on weekday afternoons," she says. "Last Monday, Sister Patricia stood underneath the Drostdy Arch for half an hour waiting for these students to arrive."

She peels her right hand off the microphone and lifts its index finger. Sunspots cluster on her knuckles.

"One came. *One*."

Someone forces a cough in the back of the church. At the lectern, Father's head hangs down, his mouth ajar, as if waiting for a plover to pick at his teeth.

"I understand if you're busy," she continues, "but you made a promise. These children are used to being let down. You are compounding this through your neglect."

She calls for a meeting of volunteers after Mass. I feel like I should go and offer to help out, but I realise the shifts clash with dining-hall lunch. Sister stands aside to let Father call the end of Mass. He sings the final hymn. It is in Xhosa. I know the tune, but I do not know the words. This seems apt. Sister follows Father and the servers as they shuffle from the altar down the aisle. She settles at the back, waiting by the holy water. One by one, the members of the congregation slide from the old oak pews, dip their hands in the pewter bowls, genuflect, and shuffle droop-headedly past her.

Outside the mist has thickened. The bells ring arrhythmicly. I look around for a group of people to walk through town with, to deter the men who would happily stab me for my dead-batteried cellphone in the darkened alleys off High Street – but I see no one walking eastward. The rest of the congregation disperses into the street and into their cars. A student shuttle illuminates the street from up the hill. I consider conning the driver into letting me hitch a ride back to the university. I could say I forgot my student card, but I doubt I would be able to pass for a student anymore.

Soon I am alone. After a while, Sister comes outside, zipping up an overcoat. She could walk straight past me, as I did her, if she wants. Instead she stops, and asks if I'd like a lift home. At first I smile, but then some force stops me from accepting – guilt, perhaps, although guilt is the Catholic's natural habitat. It is the likely prospect of conversation with a lonely septuagenarian, heading out to minister to the ill, then to putter back to her two-roomed cottage in the unweeded back garden of a pious Oatlands family. She would ask me what I do for a living, which is too complicated a question for me to answer even to myself. She would then ask me what I do for fun, which, truth told, consists mainly of forcing what few friends I have to take me for long drives out on the Cradock road, so that I can pretend I'm not living through a recurring nightmare in which I re-take Stats 3 for the second time, and let my loans odometer over into six digits.

Which, I would then have to admit, is still better than feeding orphans.

I wish Sister the best for the week ahead. She nods and forces a fragile smile. I wait for her to wish me the same, but she climbs wordlessly into her single-cab bakkie and proceeds to stall it in reverse three times, each time more violently than the last. I wave when she eventually putters off, trailing a stench of burning clutch.

A hand grips my shoulder, and for some reason I am not entirely surprised. It is when I turn that I recoil: a vagrant stands before me, middle-aged, white, visibly alcoholic. His beard is grey at its tips, his moustache knotted like a pre-school girl's first plait. I look for weapons in his hands. They are empty, thankfully, except for the strap of a tote bag, which sways from his grip in a manner that suggests emptiness.

"The Lord," he announces, like a preacher on TV. That is all he says. I read the words on his bag: EASTERN CAPE DEPARTMENT OF TRANSPORT. He has the posture of a marathon runner. A man who shuffles his feet; each step a small defeat.

"Yes," I say, "I like the Lord." A stupid reply: I am literally outside a church. But I cannot think of other words to offer. Despite myself I find myself speaking in the register one reserves for a stranger's child: "Do *you* like the Lord?"

"The Lord tells me where to go," he answers. He recites a verse of scripture, from which book or text I can't place. Through the window, I see the candles inside St Patrick's being extinguished.

"I'm busy walking," he says.

"Where are you going to?" A car rolls down Hill Street. I have half a mind to flag it down. Not for myself, but for him.

"I don't know." He digs in his moustache with his finger, dislodging a few crumbs that land on his army surplus jacket. His nails are impeccably clipped. "The Lord, He tells me where to go. I just keep walking."

"Like a Johnny Walker advert," I almost say. "That's nice," I say instead. I decide to slowly turn away from the man, in the way the

American exchange students have advised me to turn from a bear, should I ever encounter one during the trip to the Cascades I will never actually take. I'll walk through town alone, I think, muggers be damned. Anything other than this conversation. As I turn, he grabs me by the shoulder again. This time he whispers and draws closer to me: "Excuse me, sir?"

My hand balls up instinctively by my side. "Yes, my friend?" I don't know why I call him that.

"I'm hungry," he says. "Do you have … any food? Or change? I haven't eaten in a long time."

"I'm sorry, my friend, but I don't have any."

"Any change?" he says, looking into my eyes. I smell fortified wine on his breath and I wince, although I realise I probably still have the smell of Communion, of muscadel and starch, souring my own. "Anything. *Anything*."

Theatrically, I pull out my front pockets. "I'm sorry," I say. I shrug his hand off my shoulder, and point at the building inside. "Maybe the church could help you if you go inside."

A breeze blows, cold air from the autumnal hinterland, but still I feel like hot nails are being pounded into me. Between us, our breath gathers into instantaneous, fleeting boas.

His eyes glass over, and he recites, "Ask, and it will be given to you." Like sister, he raises his index finger upward. "Seek," – he pushes the finger into my chest – "and you will find. Knock …" His voice trails off as if he's realised something.

"Why don't you go knock?" I ask.

He takes a step back and turns toward the church. A saccharine wave of relief comes over me. Isn't that what churches are for, anyway? To look after the vulnerable. To shelter the homeless, to assure the shaken.

To feed the orphans.

I realise the vagrant is side-eying me. He is looking at my feet. "Give me your shoes," he says.

"Huh?"

"Give me your shoes." He now points at them. I look at my shoes. Old white factory-shop trainers. Worn soles. A couple months' in them, at most. I look at his feet. His sandals look brand new.

I reason that he'll probably just sell my shoes somewhere to buy wine, but then I realise that that is probably just what I would do if I were him. Still I shake my head and back away. He keeps on pointing at my feet. "You should be grateful for those!" he shouts, his hand shaking, with a voice monstrous and echoing. I take another step back. Reluctant to instigate a chase he can't win, he turns and stumbles towards the church's stone stoep. "Be grateful for them!" He starts saying something else, too, but he misjudges the height of the first step up. He trips, then hooks his foot with his swinging bag and falls forward. His hands don't reach out in time to break his fall, his face hitting the top step with the sound of a mallet hitting a piece of steak.

"*Cunt!*" he screams, flailing his hands on the crazy-paving that leads to the front door. "Fucking *dickhead!* Jesus! Fucking! *Christ!*" His voice then cracks, as if his vocal chords have ruptured completely. A low-pitched whine comes from somewhere deep inside him. Footsteps come from inside the church. A candle dances somewhere behind the stained glass. He begins to struggle to his feet.

I do not see if he makes it inside. I have already started running, feeling the cotton of my socks catch on the grain of the pavement.

MR DIAS

FRIDAY

"Bru, you are *fucked!*"

"*So* fucked."

The George was full. The aircon was broken, and all the TVs were blaring Italian football at a volume far too loud for Terry Dias's taste. He sat with Philip and Simon and Cristo, the four of them filling the length of the bar, uniformed in baggies and Quiksilver T-shirts, much as they did every time they went.

"Bru, those darkies are going to ship you off as quickly as they can." Philip clutched his fourth draught of Hansa.

"Surely they've gotta keep, you know, some of *us* there," Terry said, deep-throating his third. Ferreira's, the company Terry had worked for his entire career, had been bought by CMG, a national conglomerate. Now they were restructuring, and he had to re-interview for his job on Monday.

"Wouldn't count on it, bru." Cristo had his moustache in a tiny glass of grappa, which he had convinced the George to start stocking a month ago. "I heard from Mark – you know Mark from the gym?"

"Uh, ja," Terry said, scratching at his sleeve. "I think so."

"Well, Mark said his brother and his colleagues were all laid off, no pay, no severance – no nothing, hey – and the new management put in a bunch of black okes and charous in their place, and they're running it into the ground."

Simon hummed through his rum. "That was the shopfitting place, hey Cris?"

"Ja, it was those shopfitting guys. So now these new okes, right? Typical darkies, they just get tenders from their mates in government." Cristo looked over his shoulder, then up and down the length of the bar. "And even then they still can't run the business."

Terry picked at the varnish peeling off the counter. His wife, Tanya, had told him a similar story earlier over a plate of spaghetti bolognaise. They had been married twenty-two years, and she hadn't worked for the last fifteen of them. Not that she didn't want to, and not that he had discouraged it: she had had a lucrative job at the hospital on uMhlanga Ridge, setting up EEGs, the only thing she was qualified to do. That was until her favourite patient – a pigtailed five-year-old with the same freckled button nose as her own daughter – died from a brain tumour, under her care. Afterwards, Tanya had stayed in bed for a week, with the blinds drawn and Tarryn cuddled up with her. Eventually she was laid off. By then, though, Terry had been promoted from the floor to Assistant Head of Buying. A comfortable enough job – healthcare, pension, a company Camry – to let Tanya spend her days packing lunches and drinking at book club meetings in Mount Edgecombe.

"I'm just worried, now that Marie got laid off," she had said on hearing about the re-interview, in their dining room full of steam and citronella.

"I'm sure that's probably an exception," he had said to her then, grasping her hand, thumbing the diamond on her wedding band. And it was the same thing that he said to Cristo, although now his fingers were clamped around a condensing glass of beer.

"Bru," Cristo said, finishing his grappa with a flourish, "It isn't. You know Phil, hey?"

"This Phil?" Terry asked, pointing to the man sitting next to him.

"*No*, man. I mean Phil from the Greek place on Broadway." Terry shrugged, but Cristo continued anyway. "Phil's brother makes road signs. He's got this huge factory in Mossel Bay, right, with like a few dozen workers. All darkies, right?"

Terry nodded.

"And the Cape government puts out a tender to make all the road signs for the province, hey." Cristo fanned out his fingers. "Like, R10 million."

"Uh-huh." Terry signalled to the teenager working the taps for another draught.

"So Phil's brother, right, he puts together this quote for R10 million because that's what it will cost, right? But this black woman – this BEE woman, right? – with no experience, puts forward a R15 million quote."

"Uh-huh."

"So, Phil's boet's quote is cheaper, right? But you know what happens?"

"I can guess."

"Ja, you can!" Cristo said, triumphant. "Obviously the gov-ah-*munt* chooses the more expensive one."

"No," Simon and Philip chorused.

"Because she's black, hey. Government isn't allowed to choose the white man with more experience!"

"That's ridiculous," Terry said, giving twenty rand to the bartender, although he realised as soon as he said it that Cristo would misunderstand what exactly he thought was ridiculous.

"That's not the worst of it." Cristo lowered his voice as if he were about to tell a ghost story. "So you know what happens next? The woman who got the tender sub-contracts Phil's brother to do the job, and she pockets the difference."

Simon slapped his hand on his thigh. "You're kidding!"

Terry raised an eyebrow. "I'm pretty sure that's illegal."

"Bru," Cristo said, "I *swear*."

Philip gripped Terry by the bicep. "It's true, bru. I know Phil." Satisfied, Cristo hunched his shoulders and ordered another grappa. A chain, thick and gold, tumbled out from his collar. Terry turned on his stool to face the TV, and considered his fresh draught.

"Stuff the previously disadvantaged," Simon said to Philip, jabbing him in the ribs. "We're the currently disadvantaged."

"Isn't that the truth."

Terry put the beer to his lips and finished it in five quick gulps.

SATURDAY

"Pass, you shit! *Pass!*" Philip was folded into the creases of Terry's front-room couch. "He always takes two steps from the ruck before he passes. Every time."

"Boy can't play at scrumhalf. Telegraphs everything he's gonna do." Terry stood at the patio door, tongs in hand, alternating his gaze between the TV and the Weber. "It's just no good."

Saturday at the Diases: lager, rugby and four species of meat. The wives, Tanya included, huddled in the kitchen, fixing up gin fizzes and salads – Greek, three-bean, potato, coleslaw. The rest of the men were sitting on beanbags pilfered from Tarryn's room. A mosquito coil burned at the window, perilously close to the billowing lace curtain.

"Lucky it's just Scotland today." Simon drained his tallboy and burped. "We'll lose against the next decent side we play."

"We're lucky we didn't lose today," Rishi said, stepping outside for a cigarette. Rishi was the only Indian man Terry could genuinely call a friend. They'd known each other since high school; when they were the second-string lock combination, when they were both tall and fit. Unlike Terry, Rishi still played rugby, and paired his physique with vests and boardshorts, even though he never surfed. The rest of the men called him Raj, because they found it funny.

"It's that new centre pairing we have," Cristo said, rubbing at his weekend stubble. "Quota players."

"Come on," Rishi said, lighting the second-last Pall Mall in the pack. "Zwandile didn't have a bad season, and he's solid on defence. Besides, who else would you play?"

"Like, a million other guys."

"Like?"

"Swart, for one."

"Are you actually a moron?"

Terry ignored the argument, sticking a toothpick through the skin of a whorl of wors on the grill, letting the fat gush out onto the flames. A siren blared from the speakers inside. A crowd cheered. A game finished.

"Kif, bru. Whatever." Cristo heaved himself up to grab another can of beer from the kitchen.

"Hey Raj," piped up Philip from his beanbag, "speaking of quotas, did Terry tell you what's happening down at his work?"

Rishi turned to Terry and slapped him on his arm. "What's up, man?"

Terry turned the meat. "So, you know how we were bought out?"

"Ja?"

"Ja, well, turns out I have to re-apply for my job. The new management wants us to get a higher BEE rating, so, you know." He winked at Rishi. "Some of us have to go."

"That's hectic. But you should be OK, hey?"

"I dunno, Raj. Honestly, I dunno. A lot of guys have been there a lot longer than I have." Terry prodded a chicken leg with a fork to see if it was cooked all the way through. It wasn't.

"But you could, I mean, touch wood" – Rishi rapped his knuckles on the edge of a pot plant – "you could get another job."

"I don't *want* another job, Rish. I'd never be paid as much anywhere else." He pierced another piece of chicken. "And, I mean, Tarryn goes to varsity next year, and–"

"It's not good timing."

"Ja."

Rishi finished his beer. "Want anything from the kitchen, man?"

Terry shook his can, the ring pull rattling inside it. "Make it whiskey."

"I mean, you could totally pass for a coloured oke."

It was six by the time they sat at the table by the pool. The mynahs were passing over the back lawn to the trees, searching for their nests. Trails of smoke from the coals petered out over the yard. Tanya had laid out a set of cerise placemats and paper serviettes she had bought that morning, along with the sauces and salad and platters of charred, unrested, bleeding steak. She'd set out crystal goblets, but no one was drinking wine.

Terry stopped spooning salad onto his plate. "*What?*"

"Think about it," Cristo slurred. "Look at that tan. You're a Porra."

Terry chuckled. "And you're a greaseball Guido."

"No, I swear, Ter. Look, bru – look!" Cristo pointed at the TV through the sliding door. "Check Bryan Habana there. You're as dark as he is." Terry turned. He saw he was indeed as dark as the rugby player on-screen. Unthinkingly he touched his face, his skin like khaki, rough and rich.

"*And*," Tanya said, winking, "Bryan Habana has a white wife."

Terry smiled back at his wife. "Ja, no, Cris. Not a terribly good idea."

"But what do you have to lose?"

"My job?"

"Ja, but you're going to lose that anyway." The table fell silent. Cristo cleared his throat. "I mean, let's be honest, Terry. They're going to ship you out with the rest of the whites."

"That's an unsporting assumption," Rishi said, his voice almost a shout. "Cooper's restructured a couple years ago, and our department is still mostly white. Apart from me, there's only like two other Indian guys on my floor. Two Indian guys." He grimaced. "In a company in *Durban?* Come on."

Cristo turned his shoulder towards Rishi. "Ter, the only way they're going to let you keep your job is if you're black. Or coloured. Just not white, you know?"

"How can you be so sure of that?" Philip stabbed at a section of wors on his plate. "I mean, you work for yourself, Cris."

"That's irrelevant. I mean, Ter, do you think they keep records on whether you're black or white?"

"Not as far as I know."

Cristo slapped his hand on the table. "So there you go! Just mark it down that you're coloured and you'll be sorted."

Simon laughed. "I say go for it. Those BEE guys lie all the time anyway."

Terry reached an arm towards his wife. "Tan, could you pass the potato salad, please?" He looked to the rest of the table, smiling, trying to dispel the strange spirit that had fallen upon the table. "I've been doing this Banting, low-carb thing for a while, so potatoes are heaven to me right now."

Philip took the bait. "Don't get me started on *that* shit!" Terry laughed as riposte, and signalled for everyone to eat. And they sat there, the men and their wives, all in their conversations, about the rugby, their food, the weather, their friends. All except Rishi, who drank in silence, now and then heading to the kitchen for beer, letting the cans pile up in front of him.

"Hey Rish," Terry said to him as he got up a fourth time, "'S the meat all right? You've hardly touched anything."

"Ja, no, it's good actually." Rishi stood in the doorway, swaying slightly, rubbing the rubber sole of his slop against his heel.

"You OK?"

"Ja," Rishi said. "Just" – he lifted a fist to his mouth – "I need to be square with you about something. What you were saying earlier – I really don't think that's a good idea."

"What's not a good idea, Raj?"

"Pretending you're coloured." The table fell silent. Tanya dropped her fork, accidentally, and swore at herself.

"Bru, you know I'm not going to." Terry chuckled. "Who on earth would even think about trying something like that? It's such a stupid idea."

"*Stupid*, hey?" Cristo sat up straight. "You know what's really stupid?"

"What, Cristo?" Rishi leaned on the doorframe, bracing himself the short man's wisdom.

"BEE."

"And why's that?" said Rishi, his eyes swivelling around, his shoulders slouching as if already defeated. "People sometimes need a bit of a hand up. Black okes get eaten alive in the corporate world."

"Ja," Philip said, "but they have the power now."

"I'm sorry. It doesn't just work that way. You don't just get into power and everything's OK. White ous ran this country for themselves for how long?"

"That's pretty racist, Raj." Cristo laid his cutlery down.

"Ja," Philip said. "That's pretty unfair. You can't just do tit-for-tat."

Rishi exhaled and waved his can at Cristo. "You know what's unfair? How white ous don't want to share any of the spoils. You don't know what it's like to be Indian or black or coloured."

"Hey, hey, Rish." Terry held out his palm. "Yes I do. Or, you know, I can imagine. It must be hard."

Rishi smirked. "It's not *hard*. It's pretty easy to be Indian, bru – you're kinda born that way."

Tanya laughed, but quickly realised she shouldn't have.

Rishi sat down on the bench next to Terry, putting his hand on his shoulder. "Imagining's not really the same thing as knowing, you know."

"But we're all just the same," Philip said. "You know race isn't a thing. Like, literally. You know that, Rish."

"Ja." He slurped loudly from his can. "Biologically or whatever. But we don't have the same experience in life, you know."

Terry bit on his gums. He hoped Tanya would take the relative calm between the men as an opportunity to clear the plates and to fetch the pastéis she spent the afternoon baking. Cake, Terry thought. Everyone's brought together by cake. Or so he hoped. He tried to catch her eye, to communicate to her to get a move on.

But Cristo had only been biding his time. "The way you say things, you'd think whites have had it all good recently since, you know, ninety-four. But things have never been so bad." He leaned over the table, the collar of his shirt undone. "Do you know why I work for myself, Raj?"

"Do tell, Cristo."

"Because I can't get a job."

"Bull*shit*, Cristo!" Rishi cackled.

"Don't tell me it's bullshit, Raj. It's my life. No one wants to hire whites in this country. It's reverse racism."

"Tell me," Rishi said, "do you see white men living on the streets, Cristo?"

"What does that have to do with anything?" Simon chimed in.

"Just answer me."

"There's one on Mackeurtan," Simon offered, "or Tambo Road, or whatever the ANC renamed it. He begs by where that photo shop used to–"

"OK, so that's one." Rishi held up an index finger, a gold band tight around it. "Have you ever seen a white township?"

"There's one in Gauteng," Phillip piped up. "There were photos of it on the BBC."

"OK, ja." Rishi's digit stayed erect. "So that's one of them, too."

"One is still too many," Cristo said, folding his arms, with the tone of a man declaring checkmate.

"True," Rishi said, folding his own arms, "but I'm not arguing that. And shouldn't that should be true for everyone? One black township is one too many."

"Ja," Simon declared, "but that's the way it's always been. There are so many more blacks."

"Look," Cristo addressed the entire table, his arms aloft. "That's why I vote for the opposition. They don't believe in this colour crap. In this affirmative action, BEE kak. I don't care about colour. I don't see colour."

"Except when you make jokes about Indians," said Rishi.

"Ja, but they're jokes!" Simon chuckled. "You know, for fun. And you make jokes about white okes all the time."

"Ja," Rishi said, "but that's different, it's–"

"It's double standards, that's what it is, Raj!" Cristo's face had reddened. "What right do other people have to come and take jobs on the basis of their skin colour?" Bits of feta shot out of his mouth. "It's *shit*, that's what it is!"

Terry began stacking the side plates. "OK, Cris," he said. "That's enough."

"No," Rishi said coldly, "*that's* bullshit. No one's taking your job. No one *took* your job, Cristo."

"You're deluding yourself, Raj! They *are* taking jobs, and it's not fair. And that's all I want: an equal–"

"I said that's *enough!*" Terry slammed his fist down on the table, knocking condiments and glasses over. The backyard fell quiet, save for the clicking of the pool pump and the sounds of the men breathing deeply, letting out air like aerosol. Somewhere high above them, an ibis cawed, signalling dusk.

"Listen, Terry." Rishi placed his hand on Terry's shoulder. "Thanks for your hospitality, as always. And you too, Tanya." He stood and picked up his keys. "But I think I'd better go home. Karen is waiting for me." Terry nodded without speaking.

"Come on, Raj," Cristo said. "Can't you debate like an adult?"

"Fuck off, Cristo."

Tanya smiled at Rishi. "Can I tempt you to stay? With a fresh pastel de nata? I know they're your favourite."

"Afraid not, Tan, thank you." Rishi headed inside the house, his slops scuffing on the tiles. "Could you just open the gate for me, please?"

By the time Tanya came back to the table, having watched Rishi's car disappear into the broadening dusk, Terry was back in the kitchen, fixing himself another drink.

SUNDAY

"Ag, shit." Terry looked at the screen of his phone.

"What's up?" Tanya had a drawl in her voice like olive oil. Sunlight ached through the French blinds.

"I just missed an email."

"What's it say?" She shifted under the sheets next to him.

He read, aloud and atonally:

Dear Mr Dias,

I hope this finds you well.

This is a reminder that your interview with the CMG board will commence at 9:15am tomorrow at Head Office, 83 Armstrong Avenue, La Lucia.

As we have a lot of interviews to get through on Monday, we ask you to fill out and return the attached info sheet, along with your most up-to-date review and CV, by this coming Sunday evening.

The interview will be chaired by Mr Sizwe Dlamini, with Ms Karen Naidu and Dr Zika Hlatswayo also in attendance. Their profiles are on the company website, should you feel the need to familiarise yourself with the panel.

Have an enjoyable weekend.

Ms Sandra Govender
Secretary, HR, CMG (Pty) Ltd

Tanya rubbed her eyes. "When'd she send it?"

"Friday afternoon."

"Huh," Tanya said, casting the patterned sheet aside, "It's just as well you checked."

Terry could taste brandy at the back of his throat. He got up to brush his teeth, and begin his typical Sunday routine, consisting of a long shower, half an hour watching sports highlights, placing an order with the supermarket-bound Tanya for a dozen rolls, and frying platefuls of back bacon, sunny-side eggs and pan-blistered tomatoes, all while pleading with Tarryn to join them in eating it all. Then, an argument over the dishes, which invariably Tanya would win, and an argument over who would drop off Tarryn at the beach – in which Terry triumphed this week.

"Well, if I have to go to the beach," Tanya sighed, unable to take defeat lying down, "I may as well take a walk on the promenade. Make it worth my while."

"Suits me fine," Terry said, scrubbing the last pan in Sunlight and warm water. "I have to do this thing for the interview anyway."

Tanya blew him a kiss and disappeared, presumably with Tarryn in tow. He arranged the dishes in the rack, then boiled the kettle. He made a cup of instant coffee with skim milk, which he carried to the computer in his beech wood study. Leaning back in his fraying office chair, he re-read Ms Govender's message, her signature embedded at the end like a pubic hair stuck onto a bar of soap.

He clicked open the form he was to send to her. It seemed simple. On the first page, the usual: name, sex, ID, date of birth, address, phone number, email. He scrolled as he blew the steam from his mug. Surely they would have all this on file?

The second page gave him pause. How long had he been working for the company? What position did he fill? What was his income?

What "population group" does he fall under?

So they *do* care about race, Terry thought. There were five options for responding to the final question – "Black", "White", "Indian", "Coloured", and "Other", with a large check box next to each. Terry noticed how all the labels were encased in quote marks, as if trying to distance themselves from their accusatory taxonomy. What, Terry thought, would constitute an "Other"? A Chinese man? A Hispanic man? A Portuguese man – or a Lusitanian, or whatever they call us? Were Hispanic men white men in this country or were they "Other"?

Depends on whether they were from Spain or from Mexico, he supposed.

Terry took to researching his interrogators on the company webpage. He read in snatches, his eyes jumping between the three biographies. "Mr Dlamini was born in uMbogintwini in 19–" … "she graduated cum laude from the MBA programme of the University of Kwa–" … "has contributed to the *Mercury*, the *Mail &–*" … "nominated Businesswoman of the Year by–"…

He blew on his coffee again when a sentence in Naidu's profile caught his eye: "Chairperson of the National Black Empowerment Society." Pursing his lips, he scanned Dlamini's: "Mr Dlamini," he read, "is the Acting CEO of the Black Business Bureau, a body dedicated to foregrounding, synergising and advancing the causes of black businesspeople and businesses in South Africa." Terry could feel the mug's handle sliding in his grip. He took a gulp of coffee. The heat stung the back of his throat. Grimacing, he noticed a thin, solid brown ring stained on the inside of the porcelain.

He then read about Hlatswayo. Born in Lusaka to parents in exile. Educated at Wits and Harvard. The Founder of Manje Neyethu Propriety Fund, which held a majority stake in CMG. Aha, Terry thought, a big cheese, a proper businessman. Someone who would speak his language. Someone who could cut through Dlamini and Naidu's empowerment talk. Someone who would see the value he could bring to the company.

He wondered, as he usually did when he came across strange names, what the phrase "Manje Neyethu" meant. He thought it was pretty. Lyrical. He wrote the words into a translation prompt, then sat upright.

The phrase shone back at him, in all its archaic phrasing: *And so, it is ours.*

In the afternoon, Terry tended to the garden, pulling the dead fronds from the palms out front, clearing the pool pump, pressure-hosing the patio. Tanya ordered bunny chows from the Chip 'n Ranch. She and Tarryn ate sugar beans with vinegared carrots. He ate mutton with his hands.

At eight, Tanya and Tarryn sat down to the movie, while Terry went to his study and stared at the form, incomplete and unsigned on his monitor. He decided to type quickly, in case he lost his nerve.

He clicked "send" and went to bed.

MONDAY

Arriving, Terry realised Head Office had been renovated since he'd last been summoned there. New gates planted on the spine of Armstrong Avenue. Glass replaced by hand-distressed wood. A lick of paint, stone and beige. Inside, in the cold and refined air, Terry saw the new CMG logo, cast, gold-plated and fastened onto the furthest wall, each letter hanging above the receptionist's head like a trophy.

Govender's voice was airy, her blouse printed with yellow peonies. "Morning, Mr Dias," she said, flicking through her diary. "You're scheduled for …"

"Nine fifteen," he said.

She smiled. "Yes, nine fifteen. You're a bit early." She gestured over to the leather couch at the side of the room. "Just take a seat for now. I'll call you when you need to head upstairs."

"Thanks."

"Oh, and you can help yourself to coffee if you want." Terry did – two spoonfuls and three sugars in a squat black enamel mug – before sinking into the couch. He yawned incessantly. His eyes were bleary, his thoughts burdensome. He stared at a TV mounted on the wall, showing yesterday's cricket. He picked up a copy of the *Mercury* from the side table and tried to read a story about land claims on the front page, but his eyes kept reading the lead, over and over. The words became strange, squiggles distant from their meanings.

"Mr Dias!" Govender sung his name like a doorbell. "You can head upstairs now. Boardroom 2 – you know where it is?"

"Ja," he said. "Thanks."

"Good luck!" she carolled. Terry wanted to say that he would need it as he stepped into the corridor to the stairwell. The tiles were buffed, reflecting the strip lights in the ceiling. The offices he passed on either side were empty of people. He wondered where they were. At home, probably, waiting for their own interviews, their own judgements.

The noise of hard soles on wood came from above. As he reached the staircase, Terry saw a man descending, a man he had never met before, young and dark and broad and muscular, his white teeth gleaming in his beard. Grey suit. Red silk tie. Freshly-shaven head. The kind of man you see on TV selling life insurance. He winked at Terry. Terry tried to wink back, but could only blink.

They met halfway on the stairs. "Here for the interview?" the man asked, gripping the balustrade firmly. "Ja," Terry offered. The staircase was narrow, and he pushed past the man. "Sorry," he said, "Don't want to be late." The man turned, smiling at Terry as he took the steps two at a time, the seams of his trousers straining to take the pressure of his strides.

Terry arrived at the top slightly out of breath, but thought he needed to maintain momentum. To maintain purpose. He strode to the boardroom door, gripped the handle, and pushed his entire weight against the solid oak. He would enter, determined, powerful, visibly impressive and indispensible.

He pressed his shoulder against the wood, which yielded more easily than he thought it would. His shoes lost their grip, and he twisted and fell into the room, his hand still on the handle. A pen fell from his pocket and clattered on the floor, spinning on its axis until Terry picked it up, swearing under his breath.

Dusting himself down, he jerked upright. There were the three of them, partially silhouetted against the window: Dlamini, Naidu, Hlatswayo, their names engraved on little stands in front of them, on the long table at the other side of the boardroom.

"Are you OK?" Naidu asked, her voice sour.

"Ja," Terry said, closing the door. "I mean," – he cleared his throat – "yes ma'am, thank you." He paused a moment, unsure of where to put himself. "Sorry, that wasn't the best entrance."

"You must be Mr Dias," Hlatswayo said. "Come, come – sit down. That door is a bit of a nuisance. It's those new hinges." Terry shuffled to a wooden armchair, shaped as a truncated pew, which creaked as he sat in it. He eyed his interviewers, who themselves stared down at their papers. Files were stacked like pancakes next to them – one for each of the people they would speak to.

"So Mr Dias," Hlatswayo went on, "thanks for coming through today, and making time for us on such short notice." Terry saw that Hlatswayo also wore a grey suit and red tie.

"Not as if I had any choice, Mr Hlatswayo."

"I suppose not, Mr Dias. I suppose not!" The room filled with soft laughter.

"I suppose we should fill you in on what we're doing today," Naidu said. "We don't have much time, but this interview is really just a formality. We have initial reports from your seniors and superiors, as well as the information you sent us." She held up a facsimile of Terry's form. "So we don't really need to know too much more about your work life."

Dlamini rolled his shoulders, and looked Terry in the eyes. "We just need to get a feeling of who you are, personality-wise."

"To be perfectly upfront with you," Hlatswayo chimed, "we're already ninety-five per cent sure that you'll be a good fit. Most of the people in your department are, in fact. It's a major reason why CMG decided to buy out Ferreira's in the first place."

Terry smiled at this. "So you're just checking to see that I'm not crazy?"

Hlatswayo chuckled. "Pretty much." Terry's shoulders relaxed. He liked this Hlatswayo. He liked how even and deep his voice was, how his hands were adorned only with a gold wedding ring. Golfer's wrists. The kind of man who played a mean short game, refined over hundreds of meetings on the courses of the North Coast. Zimbali. Mount Edgecombe. Simbithi.

Naidu cleared her throat. "I suppose what we'd like to hear from you in particular is how you feel about your department. It says here you've been at the company for over fifteen years. You must be happy there?"

Terry nodded. Softly he recounted the years he had spent, working honestly and with determination, to pick himself up after struggling to get into university, and to find something he could be good at; to better himself and earn a good wage with which to raise a small family; to own his many mistakes and faults, and to work on them in hope of becoming a better person; to commit wholeheartedly to the work he was given; to find the quiet dignity that work afforded him and so many other people; and how, on all of these counts, he felt he had more or less succeeded, in his own small ways. And the three businesspeople on the other side of the table mm-ed and ah-ed, and smiled, and gave minute indications that they knew the things he had struggled with; that they knew these were universal hopes; and these kind of accomplishments, while modest, were not always guaranteed, certainly not today, and certainly not in this country.

"You're a company man indeed," said Dlamini. He rubbed his nose. "You know, I work on many boards, of many organisations, and see many employees of many companies. And, in my experience, the people who work best, the kind of people we need most in good companies, in this turbulent climate, are dependable, honest people, who know who they are, and who they work for. Do you think you are that kind of person, Mr Dias?"

"I certainly hope so, Mr Dlamini." Terry smiled and looked down at his lap in a manner he hoped was bashful. "I certainly hope so."

Looking at his trouser leg, he noticed a coffee stain.

"Good, good." Dlamini smiled, then started upright and looked at his watch. "We running out of time, Mr Dias, so let me just tell you quickly how the restructuring is going to happen, should all go well." And Dlamini spoke about the liquidation of assets, the redistribution of equity, turnarounds, and other things about which Terry was generally ignorant. He caught himself staring in the middle distance, toward the sunlight between Dlamini and Hlatswayo's considerable bulks.

"I have to admit, Mr Dlamini, that a lot of this goes over my head."

"That's totally fine, Mr Dias. Not a lot of it applies directly to you, but you'll get to know the most important things as they happen. Your job should remain more or less the same."

"Great," Terry said, allowing a broad smile to grow from deep within him. "That's very reassuring." How less intimidating these people seemed in the flesh, he thought, the men in their suits, and Naidu in her blue crinoline blouse and her hair bunned up. Dlamini scribbled something in his notebook. Hlatswayo had his bifocals on, looking in a file, frowning slightly, scratching at his greying temple. Terry's heart quickened. "Is there anything else I can help any of you with?" he offered.

"I don't think so, Mr Dias," Naidu smiled. "If my colleagues agree, you're free to–"

"Just a moment," Hlatswayo said. Terry stiffened. "I just have a quick question for Mr Dias."

"What is it?" Terry asked, although he already knew what he was going to be asked. Hlatswayo held up the form. "You must forgive me, Mr Dias, I might be about to embarrass myself here."

"It's OK," Terry mumbled.

"Well," Hlatswayo said, "It says here on the information sheet, the one you sent to Ms Govender yesterday, that you are – forgive me for being blunt – coloured."

Terry nodded. "It does." Naidu and Dlamini shuffled through their papers to their copies of the form.

"Oh," Naidu said, "I hadn't noticed *that*."

"Now," Hlatswayo continued, "as you would know, South African law dictates that we are not allowed to discriminate against any employee, or potential employee, on the basis of their skin colour, or their age, gender, HIV status, et cetera, et cetera." Terry nodded, although he couldn't decide whether he did, in fact, know it.

"But under the CMG constitution, there are provisions for us to ask you – and you are in no way obligated to answer – whether your stated racial category is, in fact, based in reality."

"It has important implications for our Black Economic Empowerment rating," Dlamini said.

"So, Mr Dias" – and with these words, Terry's world condensed into this small office, with its four chairs and one table, and the four people around it, and the vast window with its sea and hill views, and the blasting aircon, and the glasses of water in front of him, and the heartbeat and heat throbbing in his head, its noise audible to him over Mr Hlatswayo's voice – "do you identify as being coloured?"

Terry didn't hestitate. "No," he said. "I'm don't. I'm not."

"Ah," Hlatswayo said. Almost contentedly, Terry felt. "That was my hunch." He pulled at his collar and straightened his tie. His eyes were narrow, the pupils in them so dark they seemed to absorb the light around them. "I do need to ask you now: did you *knowingly* answer this question incorrectly?" He tilted his head and furrowed his lips.

Terry realised Hlatswayo, his imagined saviour, was offering him a way out. His back slid down the back of the chair as he assumed the posture of a thirteen-year-old. He whispered: "I can't say I didn't."

"So," Naidu said, "you knowingly wrote an incorrect answer?"

"I thought it might help."

"It most assuredly would not, Mr Dias," Hlatswayo said, his voice grave and staccato. "We take these things very, very seriously. We have to. It's the law."

Dlamini's mouth hung visibly agape. "How did you think that would help, Mr Dias?"

"I–" Terry looked out the window again, past his interrogator's shapes, to the construction sites lower down the ridge, to the ships and the waves under the droning sun. He thought about the explanations he could give, but as he rolled them in his mind, they dissipated as if scribbled in chalk. He turned to Dlamini. "I don't know," he said blankly, and knew at once that he was telling the truth. "Honestly, I don't know why I wrote that." Hlatswayo and Naidu met each other's gaze. Dlamini scribbled in his notebook.

"Well," Hlatswayo said, "this will be the cause of some deliberation." He paused, then sighed. "Do you have anything further that you would like to ask us?"

Terry shook his head. He felt the walls close in. Vertigo.

"Well, Mr Dias," Naidu said, shaking her papers. "You're free to go." Wordlessly, Terry stood and walked to the door, which he swung back on its loose hinge so that it slammed and shuddered against the wall. He jogged back down the stairs, the tips of his shoes pinching his toes all the way through the corridors, until he arrived back at reception.

"How did it go, Mr Dias?" Govender asked in her sing-song voice.

"Fine," Terry choked out. He could see another man, also white, humming and examining his phone, sitting on the same couch. "Ja, fine, thanks. I'm just going to head out. In a rush."

"Sure thing, Mr Dias." Govender waved at him absent-mindedly. "Have a wonderful day."

Terry ran out the door and across the parking lot to his car. He raced back down Armstrong, yearning for home. At the intersection near La Lucia Mall, he sat in congestion with the radio on, the voices from the broadcast filling his mind. The world outside seemed blurred, pointillist. He directed the aircon at his face.

Approaching a traffic circle, he saw an Indian man in sandals selling fruit, with a hand-painted sign leaning against his shins: NATAL LITCHIS – FRESH AND JUICY. In his hands he held lush, ripe bushels, their leaves and stems attached and bound with string. Terry pulled off onto a patch of gravel across from the Nando's where the minibus taxis normally waited. He called the vendor over and bought a bunch without haggling. Forty bucks.

Terry turned off the ignition, rolled up his window, and considered the plump, sweet fruit in his lap. Sustenance. He had no place to put any rinds, so he thought he would eat a couple the way he did when he was a child, biting directly through the hard, knobbly skin to the supple, sugary flesh beneath. He twisted a brown lump from its branch, and expertly broke the rind with his teeth. Then he gagged. Hot, fermented juice squirted into his mouth as if from an abscess, coating his tongue and gums in sour rot. He spat the fluid out onto himself and, as it began to soak into his shirt and waft up to his nose, he started to retch.

He opened the car door and hung out, half-harnessed by his seatbelt, and wondered for a moment what he had done to deserve his life. Even so, he wasn't surprised when the men by the rank, vacating the buses and taxis on their way to work, cheered as he threw up onto the dust beneath him.

RESTAURANT

Thembile had already fired the front-of-house by the time the young couple drifted in. No need for a maître d' at a customer-less bistro. But here were two, blond and flushed, shaking droplets off their umbrella onto the terracotta tiles.

She extracted herself from her corner booth, still a little stoned, and revealed a wine-stained smile. "Do you have a reservation?"

The woman sucked her teeth. "Mm, no. Did we need one?" On cue, the trio turned and surveyed the roomscape of tables, each naked save for unlit tealights and inch-tall salt shakers. Thembile shook her head. "Table for two, then?"

"I thought," said the man, side-eyeing his partner, "that we'd have a little look at the menu first." Thembile acquiesced, holding out a matt-laminated sheet, which the man took and held limply.

Thembile dreamed about what might follow. A best-case scenario at the end of a worst-case result. Tempted by the wild duck and samp risotto, or the sous-vide Agulhas mussel and hand-picked samphire terrine, or the trio of savoury sorbets (pork and apple, maple-fried bacon, chorizo and cacao), perhaps the couple might stay, talk softly between themselves all evening, sharing small smiles, maybe even sampling the wine list, making a dent in the stock Thembile would have to start liquidating the next morning. She chuckled internally at the thought. Liquidating the liquids. The liquid assets, staining her skin as they drained through cupped palms.

And perhaps at the end of the evening the couple might leave, charmed by this place above a parking lot on South Beach Road, with its tasteful drapes and murals, its curated soundtrack of classic maskandi, and a handful of Nag Champa in the burner. And perhaps they'd come back with friends, but, after getting out of the taxi they'd ordered from uMhlanga or Ballito or wherever they were from, to find the restaurant boarded up and Thembile long gone, back to Edendale, back to her tutting parents, with her French manicure and her unpayable bond.

The right kind of disappointment, she thought. One small solace.

The man didn't look her in the eye. "Sorry," he said, unapologetically. "Everything here's got something we can't eat."

"Allergies? Chef Eric can make accommodations."

The man cringed, perhaps with sympathy, perhaps embarrassment. "Uh, no. Thank you." His thumb searched for the release on the umbrella handle. "Perhaps some other time." As quickly as they had arrived, the couple left, no doubt to visit the Italian place just down the strip.

Thembile checked the clock, and saw it was already nine. She turned the lock as the door closed behind them. Lingering with a finger on the light switch by the driftwood reception desk, she saw her waitrons, by now an hour into retrenchment, had left their name badges and aprons in a scrunched pile.

She looked to the window and saw a branch of lightning rip over the ocean. She felt like she should feel something. She closed her eyes and pressed the switch.

"Chef! Order! One kingklip burger, one butternut fondant, one kale, one Nicoise, egg soft!"

"Sho'." Eric smiled and fired the hobs. "I didn't hear anyone come in?"

"Ja," Thembile nodded through the gap at the pass. "No one did."

"So who's the order for?"

Thembile shrugged and sniffed. "I've got the munchies. Hard. You may as well make something for yourself too." Eric looked at her, his mouth bunched and downturned, but said nothing. Thembile tapped her fingers on the metal shelf of the pass in the half-light until he took himself off to the pantry, his Chucks squeaking on the lino.

On her way back to her booth, Thembile stopped to look at her duo of framed reviews. Four yellowing stars from a reviewer from the *Courier*. Unstarred praise from the flatulent *Daily News* hack. "Real fine dining in Umdloti?", the latter asked, as if such a thing might be laughable. The reviewer had liked to rhyme his praise, even if it didn't make sense technically: "It's not all slops by the seaside, more like juicy great chops!"; "Forget boogie boards; hit up Thembi's new-age smorgasbord!"

She remembered being furious the day it came out. "Smorgasbord?" she had huffed to Eric during mis en place. "We're KZN-Med fusion, not some Scandinavian place!"

"And it was *shoulder* on special that night," he had said, cleaving off yellowtail heads like a logger. Eric was used to the reviewers on the North Coast. In his early career at the Hills, his cuisine classique had been considered pretentious by diners. "You should just open up a shisa nyama, Thembs. No one'll have any trouble with that. Meat and fire. Fucking genius."

"Don't forget the Aromat," said the back-braced sous-chef, whose preposition-laced name Thembile had never bothered to properly learn. Van den Berg-Auf der Maur. De Beer-Van den Hof. Something like that. "You'll make millions."

Thembile had thought then that perseverance would be key; that she could win over the locals, even with their unbudgeable love of panini and skinny decaf, of sweet pork ribs and butter chicken. That together, they could change the holders of the world's blandest palates. She owed it to herself, she thought, lest she defer another dream. And she owed it to Eric, whom she had headhunted from a craft beer brasserie in Musgrave. And, haemorrhaging cash, she supposed she owed it to the bank, too.

But now, about to uncork her second bottle of Vrede en Lust in the gloom, she wondered why she had put herself through it.

She heard the bell chime from the pass and left the wine. The last round of food sat plump and fresh upon six gleaming ceramic plates under the heating lamp. She looked around for dishcloths to pick them up, and found two discarded on the floor. As she carried the first two plates to her table, she heard a scooter engine fire up from the lot. She didn't need to check who it was. She could see Eric had left the back door open.

She read the Huletts sugar packets as her self-poured Dom Pedro, made with the last dregs of a bottle of Tullamore DEW, cooled. Platitudes printed on brown paper, encasing sunsweet brown sugar, burned and hand-extracted from fields not twenty minutes away. Coffee-time talking points. Handbag-ready encouragement. Disposable inspiration.

"'A strong person and a waterfall always channel their own path.' – UNKNOWN". Maybe, she thought, if the person who had said this was *that* strong, they'd have done something significant enough for someone to remember their name.

She tossed the packet aside, and pulled out the next. "'We are still masters of our fate. We are still captains of our souls.' – WINSTON CHURCHILL". Easy to say if you're Winston fucking Churchill.

She looked at the next sachet: '"It's better to light a candle than to curse the darkness.' – ELEANOR ROOSEVELT". For once she hummed in agreement.

She regarded the tealight in front of her, then her table, then the rest of the dining room. Twenty tables. Sixty chairs. Sixty covers, now forever unfilled.

The lightning had long since passed, heading south toward the city. In its wake, more rain. Gallons now, lashing the street, the patio, blown in streaks down the windows.

She tore open the two packets she had discarded and emptied them into her glass, scrunching up the advice, tossing it on the floor. She sipped. Not enough whiskey – not nearly enough. She swayed into the kitchen, the only room in the restaurant still illuminated, and looked for another bottle. Passing by the hobs she stopped, nostrils flaring. Gas. Lungfuls of it. Eric had left all the hobs on, unlit. Passing her eyes over the stove, she saw Eric's bottle of J&B, half-full and upright on the extractor fan. Next to it sat a fat cardboard box. A fire hazard, surely.

She took the box down from the extractor and peeled back its loose-hinged flaps. She sighed as she realised what was inside. Sugar sachets. Hundreds of saccharine snippets of advice.

The whiskey could wait. She took the box in both arms like she would a sleeping toddler, lugging it into the dining room. With her foot she pushed the patio door open, sending it humming along its tracks, and walked out onto the balcony. She thought instinctively of her hairdresser, of the instructions not to get her braids wet. But that didn't matter to her, not here, not now. In one motion, she strode to the balustrade and heaved the sachets out of the box into the carpark, all over the Mercedes and the Volkswagens and the single-cabs, their windscreens and windows glistening with shattered, sliding rain under the security lights. And then she stood, hearing the dull din of the storm and the wind and the damn Italian place somewhere in the distance, letting her scalp soak and grow heavy, and watching the paper saturate, the aphorisms melt sweetly into the street.

She stood there for a while before she returned to her booth. She left the door open. She felt like feeling the draft, the coolness, the tempest. Inside she could smell the mercaptan from the gas, an alert like sulphur, drifting in thick from the kitchen. She slouched back against the upholstery, drunk enough to forget the whiskey entirely. Her eyes adjusting to the dark again, she regarded her half-drunk coffee, the empty green wine bottles, the smeared, half-eaten plates of food, and the single, unlit tealight, sitting beside the single sugar sachet she had spared.

She scrumpled the packet in her right pocket, and extracted the off-brand Zippo from her left. She picked up the candle. She sniffed. Better this, she thought, savouring the lighter's metallic flick, than to curse the darkness.

MARIANNHILL, IN THE GARDEN

The first night, after tea, after rusks and helloes, the women gathered in the garden under the clock tower. A mist-belt Gethsemene of acacia, delicious monster, trimmed hedge. No questions were asked, no directions given. In the dark they wandered, following a teenager in a white shroud. She carried a petrified cross, barefoot on the devil thorns hidden in the gravel. Instinctively, Mary approached to help the girl carry the load. But the chaplain raised his arms, telling the women to stand back. They were not to help the girl as she dragged this cross, heavy on her back, along a path indeterminable, through the monastery grounds, under a moon like milk.

The girl didn't make a sound the first time she fell. But the second time, she yelped, and stayed on her knees for a moment, collecting herself. Mary stepped forward again, and again the chaplain raised his hand to her. In slow motion, in one motion, the girl picked herself and the cross up, and carried on through the darkest shadows of the garden. The women stumbled, unfamiliar with the terrain, in the heat of the crowd.

When the girl fell a third time, the chaplain began to sing.

Were you there when they crucified our Lord?

He barked: "Sing!"

Were you there when they crucified our Lord?

In the bus, the other women had sung the entire journey. They had sung hymns Mary hadn't heard since her childhood in the Midlothian church, all Thees and Thous, tristis et afflicta, as if Vatican II had never happened. Now the women had to be coaxed into praise.

"Everyone, sing!"

O, O-o-o! Sometimes it causes me to tremble, tremble, tremble.

Mary trembled. She would have cried, too, if she could process the thought of it. To her, this was a fresh hell, among the ferrous hills and petrichor bush of the Upper Highway.

It took six verses before the procession came to an end. Under a lit archway, a number of priests laid the girl on top of the cross. The chaplain raised his hands again, not in censure, but to silence. A monk in black robes then extracted three thick nails from a sling bag, and knelt to the girl. With a hammer, emotionless, he battered each one into the cross, as close to the girl's hands as possible. The voices ascended.

The girl wailed with each wallop of the wood and lead. Mary trusted the monk was not hitting the girl, but she couldn't be sure. With the vibrations her shroud began to shift, and she looked out at the crowd. Between the backs of the heads of the other women, the girl's face revealed itself to Mary. Bright eyes, cast straight and defiant. Scarred cheeks, bloating and sinking with each shout.

Mary counted the strokes of the hammer. The left nail took eighteen; the right, twenty-one. The monk, tiring, took the final nail, and placed it above the girl's crossed feet. One, two, rhythmic, like clockwork, like heartbeat. Three, four. In the half-light she could see the musculature of the monk's arm. The knuckle-wrapping veins, the forearm tendons like the underside of a leaf. It would be over soon, Mary thought. Perhaps soon they might get some sleep.

On the fifth stroke the monk's grip slipped, and the hammer deflected off the head of the nail into the girl's toes. A metatarsal crunch, audible over the distant cicadas. The girl stopped wailing, and grimaced instead.

Mary could see the girl's teeth were rotten. She could see that much.

∽

In the church, the cross loomed illuminated. Immediately Mary knew the monks would not be letting the women sleep yet. Before Mass, they were each given a shard of terracotta. A broken pot. In her seat in the hardwood pew, Mary rolled the shard in her hand, its roughness scraping out the miniscule valleys in the pads of her fingers.

The chaplain began a spoken Mass, smiling now. Mary eased into the routine, her brain on autopilot. Halfway through the Kyrie, she felt a ringing at her breast. Her phone, which she had been supposed to hand over to the chaplain when the bus first arrived. She snatched at it, fishing it out of her bra, searching for a button to silence it. She dropped the terracotta shard, shattering it on the stone floor. The chaplain did not stir, so she bowed her head, contrite, praying that he had not noticed.

When she stood after hearing the second reading – something from Paul's prison letters to the Philippians – she felt a tap at her shoulder. The chaplain was standing above her, his face still, his hand held out.

One by one, the women were called to confession. And as she walked out into the garden again, she felt as though her feet were lifting from the earth.

∽

During the night, Mary thought she was dying. Not a panic attack, just a conviction that the chaplain would find her on the foam mattress in the morning, lifeless. Things howled through the gaps in the putty around the window panes, around the walls outside: grief in a spiralling darkness.

Every moment Mary found herself nearing sleep, she would jolt awake with the bells, which rung for the monks' prayers every half-hour. The bells, she thought, those clarions of hell, in aid of – what exactly? The cleansing of the dark recesses of the soul, of the slurry of the heart?

She had no further concept of time, only that it was passing. No concept of herself, as she drifted between these bodily and spiritual planes.

Was this death, she thought, visiting itself upon me? What if I die here in this place, shivering in this turbulence? She imagined herself speaking to her child, and thoughts rolled unfettered through her mind. What of the works I have promised you, to the world, to myself? Who will execute them? Will you take it upon yourself to sort through the parts of me, to piece me together again from these fragments of myself, from unfinished prayers, from miscellany? Will you bear it upon yourself to make me live forever, through everything, to make of me a monument, to remind yourself of me through your last days?

And what if you find of the parts of me of which I am ashamed, my unlovable parts, the hidden parts? In death I used to believe we would come into the full knowledge of everything, that no secret could be held forever, that all deathbed betrayals would be made known, all horrors leaked – and it would be all right, for we were all capable of horrors, for we were all capable of the worst kinds of things, of things unspoken, unthought, things omitted, pretended to be omitted.

And how would you remember me? These things would not matter in death, of course, for there would not be me. There would be me and the thing we call God, in totality: no less. There is no question God exists, even if God is the void; not the beginning of the world, not the end of the world, but the middle of the world. Between genesis and apocalypse. There is no question God exists. There is no question God exists. There is only a question of what God is.

She heard chanting. Prayers with the steady insistence of pulse-beat. She sat up. Through the window she could see lines of monks – twenty, thirty of them – arms linked, walking through the garden toward the dormitory. She couldn't look away. The bell tolled.

She took a breath. She closed her eyes.

STATIONS

I

I was alive. I was dead. That's as much as I knew.

I want to tell you I woke, but I don't think I was ever asleep. I had passed through. Or something. There's no way to explain it, unless it were to happen to you.

I was disappointed at first that I couldn't walk through things, that I wasn't a ghost. I could still feel the brush of fynbos beneath me, the grit of rock against my skin. I expected to see blood, a crater, an outline of dust around where I landed. I expected to see a rope halfway up the cliff, worn through, in frays, dangling in the wind; or a cracked helmet someplace, and a chalk bag somewhere else. I looked to my hands, no longer calloused, left with no trace of chalk. I had no bruises, no bones protruding from my skin.

The sky was blue, but not a blue I had ever known before, hanging over the careering vistas of Silvermine, with the green and the scrub and the haze and the ocean, unfolding and gathering and foaming and all of it – just the same as it was before. Then I turned. The cellphone tower was gone. The buildings were in different configurations, but in which ways, I couldn't quite be sure.

Eagles circled above me. Jet streams scarred the firmament of a world silent and full. In that moment, I was glad.

II

The road down was still there, although the substation it led to wasn't. At that moment, I felt no pain, no hunger. My legs felt light, healthy with muscle – just as before, but as if all their cells had been generated anew.

Animals and plants poked through the scrub that lined the track. I'd spent a lot of time here before – but now there were things I'd never seen. These flowers – crimson ericas, three metres high. An arm-length lizard gleamed purple and green on a rock near my feet. Things that had been long dead were alive. My nose itched with strange pollen.

I imagined I was invincible. The road led to a knot of hairpins halfway down: a waste of walking if one could jump down a short section of cliff. My heart raced at the prospect of doing things without the promise of harm. A platform of sandstone jutted out about three metres down. I savoured the air on my skin as I dropped.

The soles of my feet tore as I landed. I slipped backwards, flailing my arms at the rocks, grabbing for any hold that would stop me careering down the rest of the cliff. I scrabbled near the edge of the platform, with the air and the valley expectant before me. I rubbed myself with my hands, finding new marks and scars on this body. I fingered a wound, fresh, a half-inch thick, in the side of my abdomen, throbbing and bleeding fast down my hip and thigh. I pressed my hand to it, feeling the quick heaving of my chest and the waves of pain washing through me. I panted. I breathed in dust. I thought about infection, about bacteria unknown.

Sitting back, holding my knees to my chest, I could feel the chill of the wind. I saw now that I was uncircumcised. I hunched over. I yelled.

There was no echo.

III

The pain subsided as the sun began its downward turn. I climbed from the platform to where the road resumed – ten metres, perhaps. Nothing far, but hard to climb without rubber-soled boots, chalk or clothes, even, to shield and stem the weepings of my flesh.

Only then, for the first time in years, did I think about my shade. When I was a child, my mother told me how the spirits of the dead had to be led home so they could be put to rest. I had taken it for granted that was how things worked; when I died, sometime far in the future, I – disembodied, ethereal – would be led back to the place of my birth, by whoever my wife or my children would be, and I would rest.

But the living weren't here. Sal wasn't there – on the mountain, holding the belay rope – when I realised I had fallen. What Sal would be left with wasn't me, but only what would have been left of me. A thing to piece back together; to bury someplace where someone thought I'd like to be. Home, perhaps. But there – wherever home was now – wasn't where I was, where I ever could be.

On the road down, I looked across the valley to the parklands and the buildings, all of them thatch-roofed and spread out in grids. I thought about how Mother had died, how Yia had died, how everyone I knew who had died had died: all far from home. All had needed to be carried back, to be led.

And how strange these thoughts felt, as the road levelled and I could see what lay before me.

VI

Mother, wanderer: now I know what you know. We are our own shades.

V

Everything was familiar, but not familiar enough to be comforting.

I had found a pair of white running shorts discarded on the hard shoulder. They seemed clean enough to wear, although even a rag would have done – anything to shield my nakedness from the stream of motorists labouring up Ou Kaapse Weg, or whatever it was called here. My wounds had begun to clog. I was limping. I tried to meet the eyes of the motorists who passed me, ostensibly to try and catch someone's expression, to let a smile or a frown soothe me, to let me know that this was all normal, that I would adjust.

Or to get a lift. Really, all I needed was a lift.

No one looked. No one stopped.

I was dazed, from loss of blood or vertigo – or both. The suburbs below looked as though they had been built from memory – a dream-world, something hazy and inexact, where the streets and the skylines were not quite in the right proportions or configurations. The buildings were smaller, taller, more densely packed. The golf course had been taken over by houses with hearths and chimneys and gardens. I could see no prisons, no consulates, no malls.

Halfway down, I came across a white cross leaning on a barrier by the side of the road. Someone had placed a bunch of puce azaleas under it, wilting in the sun. I tried to read the card someone had attached to the stems, but it was written in glyphs I couldn't understand.

VI

There were people at the train station: cotton-shirted women and men wearing beads like my mother's around their necks. Children stood with adults speaking as equals – in tongues both known and unknown. The boys gesticulated and the men listened solemnly: here, an adult and a child might be the same age.

I stood near the tracks as I had done a hundred times to go into the city. But I didn't know where the trains on this platform would go. The train I would have caught yesterday would have taken me from here towards Cape Town, passing Retreat, Plumstead, the bottom end of Observatory, and everywhere else I had ever lived. The stations here might be different, the routes circuitous and strange. I turned to the pair standing nearest to me – a sun-spotted elder with buttermilk skin and a teenager in slacks and a T-shirt.

"Excuse me, sir," I said to the old man, "but where is this train going, exactly?"

He looked at me, wordless.

"Ah, uxolo, tata." I tried again. "Uloliwe ... eh, uya phi?"

The man stared at the wound in my side and tilted his head, his eyes widening. He spoke like fingers clicking.

The teenager chuckled. "You're not from around here."

"You could say that."

The man was pointing at my side, raising his voice. I saw his fingers were gnarled, with growths like bark. I asked the teenager what the man was saying.

"He says you should get that cut looked at." He laughed. I didn't.

"I just want to know where the train on this platform goes."

The teenager smiled still. "Look, this train goes lots of places. Lots."

"I just want to go to town," I said.

"Town?"

"Cape Town. The CBD – you know? I want to look for people."

"CBD?" He paused for a moment. "Oh right – right. Ja, the train goes there. It's a nice ride along the sea."

"Yeah, cool," I said. "Thanks."

The pair began to walk away, resuming their conversation. "Wait," I said. "Wait, just a second, please?"

"Ja, what?"

"What about tickets?"

The teenager laughed. "You don't need tickets, man. It's a train. Just get on."

"You don't have to pay?"

"No," he said, turning from me again. "Things are paid for in other ways here."

VII

He was right – the view was nice. The air was clear, the sky abundant. The land heading north was about the same as I remembered it, littered with houses, complexes, apartment blocks.

I had expected more.

The carriage was made of wood and plastic – musty, high-ceilinged and jiggering with the camber of the tracks. I had a bench to myself, away from the people who spoke softly in odd-matched pairs, about the weather and other things I couldn't decipher. A dark man – darker than me – walked down the aisle, passing out boiled sweets from a woven basket.

Despite what the teenager said, I couldn't see the sea. It made sense. Surely one would only see the ocean heading in the direction of Simon's Town or whatever was there now. But in this direction? The stations we came to had no signs, only numerals, descending as we went towards the end of the line. A voice on an intercom spoke new names as we arrived at each. I oriented myself by tracking the rotation of the mountain through the opposite window.

When we stopped somewhere near where I thought Rosebank would be – VII – the voice said "Khayelitsha". Something in my chest began creeping, cold. This was nowhere near Khayelitsha. I peeled myself off the bench and limped over to the window. I could see nothing but the station, built three storeys high from stone and pine, with a quilt work of flags hanging from poles on the eaves. To the left and the right were subways, heading underneath a road, flanked by a frontier of willows. I saw my face in the glass. I looked the same.

The carriage jolted and sent me sprawling onto the floor. I felt the wound pulse under my ribs. I was surprised when no one laughed.

Maybe the name for this new place was apt, I thought, retaking my bench. Maybe it was a different kind of new home. A better one.

VIII

I had sat on the opposite side of the carriage, trying to look around the banks of trees as we coasted north. I was picking at a scab on my foot when the trees began to thin, somewhere near Mowbray, and the most incredible things opened up to me. Blocks of flats, towers of stone and mortar, all among the slopes and folds of Devil's Peak. Colonies of concrete favelas, houses with pitched roofs all hanging off the rock, connected by poles with wires like spider web. Funiculars climbed the slopes, humming all around and across the mountain, all pulsing with movement. Neighbourhoods unimaginable and strange – people were living not around, but on Table Mountain.

At Woodstock, columns of townhouses ran parallel from the peaks to the tracks – a disorienting parallax, opening and closing like accordion bellows. District Six, a garden city in miniature, in octagon and pentagon, lush and glowing in the sun. In every neighbourhood dozens of statues rose on plinths, piercing and needling the pink-edged sky.

The train entered a tunnel, and I peeled my gaze from the window. The carriage was now empty, save for a pair of men, shirtless in shorts, with leather backpacks on their laps. They looked like what people used to call bushmen. I'd never seen a bushman in the flesh before, only in books and Afrikaner movies, worshipping Coke bottles and tracking kudu. One mimed the action of rolling dice. The other clapped hysterically.

The tunnel echoed the clacks of the wheels and the tracks and the engine. A minute passed in the darkness, the carriage lit by a single bulb suspended from a cable bound in rope, which cast a harsh shadow of amber and orange. The men were laughing, and I caught myself staring at them, trying to decipher their rasps and snaps. And they stared back, furrowing their brows, stone silent – until I looked away again, and waited for us to emerge.

IX

But the sea. The sea, cellophane blue, crashing and crinking on itself. And empty. There was no harbour, the cresting shoreline naked of concrete or metal. Highways and high-rises had cut off the city as I knew it from the sea; from the shelter the bay gave from the squalls and the waves and the deluges of winter; from the entire reason of its existence. How naked the bay seemed now.

We followed the shore into the city bowl – except there was no city. Just small neighbourhoods, like everywhere else on the flatland, interspersed with towers and spires and statues. Smoke billowed from the top of the mountain like clouds. Signal Hill rustled with strange trees.

My heart dropped. This place had a geography that had to be relearned.

X

Later I found that the spires and the minarets I had seen from the train were just that: there were still churches and mosques and temples here, teaching the same things they always had – forgiveness, piety, fear; with scriptures retconned into interpretations that would explain this afterlife.

Although this wasn't the afterlife. This was life. Death was nothing to be feared, for this was death. What was unknowable was plainly knowable; experience, plain experience, unavoidable. And experience was knowledge. As was memory – all of it. Every iteration. Every variance.

Remember this. Number your moments like beads.

XI

The train terminated where I thought town would be. I alighted in a cavernous station: an arcade with open timber struts running its length. I left through an archway, turned left and, after a few steps, found myself on a belvedere looking over a beach. The Foreshore was gone. It had not been rebuilt, the ground not reclaimed, its streets a shimmering memory. No moorings or docks or even a pier. I supposed the slaves who had first built those things weren't in the mood to build them again.

I saw that the tracks extended past the station, towards the Atlantic seaboard. I was curious to see what would be there too. But there was no rush. I suspected I had the time.

The wind picked up. The water lapped against a stone wall below me. The sun began to dip behind the forests on the hills. Clouds gathered over the mountain. My skin grew taut.

Out the corner of my eye I saw the bushmen behind me, sauntering over Strand Street, towards a park where the Grand Parade used to be. I followed them.

XII

Cecil Rhodes sat on a taxidermied horse in a cage on a plinth in the middle of the Parade. I wouldn't have known who he was if there wasn't a sign beneath him, as if he were a stuffed animal in a museum. Old men were slinging pieces of gravel at him disinterestedly from a few metres away, one with a small catty made of rubber and knotted wood. Rhodes didn't recoil from the blows. He only swayed, blood dripping and something foaming out his mouth. His chest heaved.

He was alive. He couldn't die.

There were dozens of them, men and women, caged and shackled on pillars throughout the Parade, some neglected and bored, stroking old scars, some bearing injuries that would have meant death under other circumstances.

Truthfully? They spoiled the view. The park was beautiful, filled with sage and yellowwood and unknown shrubs, all filled with the sunset chatter of animals I'd never heard before. Families walked down the lanes. Children sat on benches and ate apples and drank from water bottles, enjoying the last sun of the day. Some of the pillars holding the cages were encrusted with the most exquisite flowers, glowing gold and fuchsia and grey, growing over dried and drying blood, obscuring the gore.

I realised then that all the plinths I had seen from the train were supporting living statues.

I also realised that if I concentrated hard enough, I could ignore the groans.

XIII

This city was saturated with memory. Maybe that's why they never rebuilt it, letting this park do all the remembering for them.

I left the park and took a right down a lane flanked with townhouses. Buitenkant. I tried to anchor myself with memories of this place. I tried to think about the days spent at the theatres and bookshops on the intersections, the parties I had stocked from the bottle store, the nights I had spent at the tavern further up the hill, eating squid, drinking clear spirits.

The statues were on every corner – supplicating people, begging to be stared at, begging to be pitied. No doubt they deserved their suffering: why would they be there otherwise?

I asked a man marked with the name of a settler why he was trapped up on his plinth.

"Wat dink jy?" he asked me. His teeth were chipped and yellow. "Dit is net wat jy sien."

"Jy was 'n slegte persoon in 'n vorige lewe," I said.

"Maar wat beteken 'slegte'?" he mumbled. "Julle mense vra al dieselfde vrae. Die wêreld bereik ewewig uiteindelik. Dis net wat jy sien."

The decades had reduced him to platitudes. I asked him if he wanted to die.

"Ek's alreeds dood."

I asked him if he wanted to die again. He was silent.

I asked a passing man why the settler was up there, forced to live in pain and resignation. He hunched his shoulders. I'm not sure he understood the question.

XIV

The foghorns began like calls to prayer, sonorous voices between the peaks and the buildings. The lights of the new villages shimmered up the mountain. The cloudbank had settled, and the streetlights and the pulsing of electricity and fire came to me in waves, unrelenting, unsettling.

This was no CBD. This was no Town. No wonder the teenager had laughed at me. I walked up the entire length of Buitenkant, between the truncated high-rises and the duplexes. On every block, there was a different living statue, in poses distorted and gnarled, accompanied by inscriptions of the sins and pains they had visited on the people with whom they had shared the world before, and with whom they were forced to share the world again. And it was as if those people had decided to move from this place, from the idea of this city, and from this city that had itself been a monument to so much pain – to so much ruin, even in its beauty. Something that had been built on bodies and bones. As if this place was a monument to everything that had come before; to those who had destroyed their past lives, in the hope they could have the lives they wanted now.

I felt I should make my way up the mountain, to see all the new things, to see what people had remade of themselves. To find someplace to stay. I could start looking for family, for friends tomorrow. I could find them in a phonebook, maybe, if phonebooks existed in this place.

I could see the funiculars in the distance, their stations beginning on the edge of Gardens. The foghorns rang again, loud and true. The streets had emptied, apart from the statues. I felt this creeping inside my chest, this electricity, constricting and hammering at me. I quickened my step.

On the corner of Mill Street, under a bridge, I came across a man – a black man in a black suit – on his haunches, checking his watch.

I said hello. He smiled at me, and I felt myself smiling back at him. Tears gathered in my eyes – for what, I couldn't be sure. I asked the man what he was doing. He said he was waiting. I asked him what he was waiting for. He said he liked to hear the music. I asked what music, and that's when they started to sing.

All the men, all the women, all the statues, all on their plinths, all in their cages. A thin trail of voices rising from the streets nearby, punctuated by the foghorns, softened by the noise of the night. They began a hymn. They sang, well-practised, well-routined, mournful:

Genade onbeskryflik groot
het U aan my bewys
verlore seun 'n wegloopkind
weer in die vaderhuis

This happened every night, the man told me, and he came out every evening to listen to them. He found it soothing; the Afrikaans words fitted the tune better than the English version he knew as a child.

I asked him why they sang.

He asked me: why would anyone sing?

Maar U sien ver, oneindig ver.
U sien my honger, dors.

The man started singing along, softly. The streetlights began to flicker on, then glowed blue.

I spotted another man not far away. A statue man, in regalia, shackled astride another stuffed horse. He was set on a wide plinth, flanked by jacarandas in bloom. He led those near him in a monstrous baritone, with his eyes closed and his eyebrows furrowed. A great thicket of beard moved with his words.

I crouched to the suited man. I spoke in a hushed voice, somehow not willing to disturb the sanctity of the hymn, no matter how grotesque its performance, no matter how futile a plea for grace might be here.

"Uxolo, tata," I said. "Ngubani na lo?"

He looked me in the eye. "Awumazi?"

I shook my head.

He grabbed my hand, still scarred and bloody, and whispered: "Botha."

"*Louis?*"

"Ja."

Want toe ek kom, my skuld bely,
druk U my aan die bors.

I stared at Louis Botha, in the same position I'd always known him, a statue outside Parliament, although that was a place that wasn't a place anymore. I wanted to say I felt comfort, but comfort isn't the word.

I felt an itch on my side and inspected my wound. A fly had landed on it. I flicked it away with a fingernail, and the wound started bleeding again. The suited man said I should get it looked at. I nodded and said goodbye, and he continued singing.

I turned to the mountain. I walked.